Killer Suburbia

Also written by C. L. Conolly

Lone Titles
Friendly Misfortunes

The Affair Series
Forbidden Affair
Family Affair
Fundamental Affair
Fruitful Affair

Killer Suburbia

C. L. Conolly

This is a work of fiction. Any references to historical events, real people, living or dead, or real places are used fictitiously. Names, characters and places are the products of the author's imagination.

Cover art by EPiC
Author photo by Julie

Printed in the United States of America

Killer Suburbia
ISBN 978-0-9886876-5-3

First Edition
www.clconolly.com

"Killing is a lifestyle. There is an intense need, as well as an excitement, when you wrap your hands around someone's throat and squeeze the life out of them. It's absolutely euphoric."

- Silas Graham

One

Silas Graham had grown up in a close knit family. His parents, even though they were busy working hard in order to earn millions of dollars each year, always made time for him and his siblings. He had one older brother, one older sister, along with one younger sister. The four children generally always got along, with little sibling spats here and there, but otherwise they always shared their secrets with each other.

He was a happy kid and a jokester, but once his body began to change and he realized he was attracted to the other boys, rather than the girls, he began isolating himself at home, trying to hide who he truly was. His siblings noticed that he was no longer sharing with them, so they approached him. They let him know they had accepted his sexuality and that it didn't change who he was to them.

That was when he realized he had violent sexual fantasies. At the age of fifteen, Silas began lifting weights and working out in order to gain confidence in himself. He had a few dates with some fellow students at his school, but when they would become intimate, Silas would wrap his hands around the other boys neck and begin choking them.

Each one of the boys would escape his grasp, then avoid him at school. None of them told anyone what happened, but that was when Silas decided he needed to find someone he didn't know. He figured if his victim was someone he didn't have a personal connection with, most likely he wouldn't hesitate when strangling.

For a couple of years, Silas took the time to perfect his approach, as well as plan his body disposal. He figured out the best ways to pick his target was to go unnoticed in a crowded room and he made the decision to travel further from his home, just to keep from being suspected.

By the time he was seventeen, he was ready to go out searching for someone to engage with and play out his sexual fantasy.

The home he grew up in sat on twenty acres, split by a creek that ran through the middle of the property. The front ten acres was where the family home was placed. It was a five thousand square foot home where each child basically had their own area; they had their own bedrooms as well as their own bathrooms and a separate lounge area for each child.

On the back ten acres, there was a one thousand square foot cabin that Silas and his siblings used as a playhouse when they were young. By the time he was planning to stalk his first victim, his two older siblings had moved out and it was just him and his younger sister living with his parents.

At that time, his younger sister was fifteen and she no longer went to the cabin to play, so he felt it would be the perfect place to bring his sexual conquest. His parents had set it up as a guest cabin in order to keep it from becoming dilapidated, but the only time anyone actually entered, was when the maid would come to clean and the pest control company would come to be sure it wasn't being taken over by critters.

In order for him to maintain his image with his target when he brought them home, Silas set up the cabin to look as though he lived there. The one main addition was hidden under the pillow in the bed, a white nylon rope to wrap around the guy's neck.

Once he was satisfied with appearances, he went back to the main house to prepare to go out. His parents weren't home when he left and his little sister was at a sleepover, so it made it easier for him without all of the questions of where he was going and when he would get home.

Silas had met someone at a car hop restaurant

where he had spotted large groups of teenagers were hanging out. He had been vetting his victim for a few months just to pique his interest.

The first couple of times, Silas would park in a spot in the back of the parking lot where he could watch the people, before deciding to choose his target. Once he had made his decision, it wasn't until his third visit that he had decided to approach his chosen one. He visited with his victim twice a week to gain his trust. During the first meeting, he found out the targets name was Luka and he had just moved to the area.

Luka was bullied relentlessly, but his parents insisted that he follow what the other kids were doing in order to gain favor with the popular crowd. Unfortunately, all it did was cause the bullying to get worse, but mostly from his parents. He preferred being around the kids who bullied him, rather than being around his parents.

Silas felt connected to Luka. It was mostly because he knew no one would miss Luka once he was gone. After a few visits, Luka came to look forward to seeing Silas. Once Silas was sure he could convince Luka to go home with him, he headed out to pick up his target.

Silas parked in the same spot he always did, exited his vehicle and walked around to lean against the bumper. He spotted Luka sitting alone at the same table on the patio. The boy was eating a basket of French fries. As Silas watched him for a few moments, Luka was hunched over the basket, slowly munching one fry at a time; nervously and nonchalantly looking around at the other people who were socializing around him. Silas smiled to himself, as he walked over to the table.

"Is anyone sitting here?" Silas asked.

"You know the answer to that question," Luka said, smiling and gesturing for Silas to join him.

"Hey, so I was thinking on my way over here, would you want to go home with me tonight?" Silas asked, as he sat down at the table.

"Is there a specific reason you want to take me home?" Luka asked, raising his eyebrows.

"I just thought it would be nice to go somewhere

we could be alone," Silas informed him.

"That might be fun. I think we could get into a little trouble if we were alone," Luka said, sitting up straight and pushing the fry basket to the center of the table.

"That's exactly what I was thinking. We could have a little fun, get into a little trouble, maybe do a few things that some people might find to be taboo," Silas said, gently touching Luka's hand.

"I have never met anyone like you before," Luka said, interlocking his fingers with Silas.

"I try to be unique."

"I think that is what has drawn me to you."

Silas felt a magnetic pull to Luka and Luka seemed drawn to him. They sat at the table and talked until the parking lot had cleared out and the employees began their closing duties. The two of them stood and headed over to Silas' vehicle together.

"Are you the only LGBTQ person at your school?" Silas asked.

"I'm the only one who is willing to admit it. I'm sure there are several jocks who deny it," Luka told him.

Silas smiled before he leaned in and kissed Luka. As their tongues wrestled, Luka slid his hand down Silas' chest and began rubbing his manhood over his pants. Silas maneuvered his hips in order to lean into Luka's touch.

"So, do you want to take this back to my place?" Silas whispered into Luka's ear, before gently nibbling his earlobe.

"Absolutely, I do," Luka replied, as he cupped his hand over Silas' bulge.

Silas unlocked his vehicle and opened the passenger door for Luka, before stepping around and climbing into the car on the driver's side. Silas cranked up the engine and drove back to the cabin.

"Where are we going?" Luka asked, as Silas headed out of town.

"I'm taking you to my house," Silas responded, reaching over to rub Luka's thigh.

"How far do you live?" Luka wondered, beginning to feel uneasy.

"It's not far, I promise," Silas told him, sliding his

hand up to Luka's crotch, trying to help him relax.

"I wish you would have told me you didn't live in town," Luka said, taking Silas' hand off his lap.

"Would you have agreed to come home with me if I told you that the drive would take about an hour?" Silas asked.

"Probably not. I figured that if I needed to, I could walk home, but I can't walk from way out here," Luka said, frantically watching the scenery pass by through the passenger window.

"Relax. I promise you won't be able to walk once we are done anyway, so just release your inhibitions and look forward to the activities we are about to engage in," Silas tried to comfort Luka.

Luka took a deep breath, sunk back into the passenger seat, then watched Silas' face for the rest of the ride. He was looking for possible sinister expressions to suggest that he could be in danger, but Silas' expression never changed.

Silas pulled up in front of the cabin and turned off the motor. He turned in his seat and looked over at Luka, who had been staring at him from the passenger seat for the past few miles.

"Are you ready to go inside?" Silas asked.

"This is farther than I was expecting," Luka said.

"Is that a problem? I like the privacy."

"I don't understand why you would keep this from me. How am I suppose to get home?"

"I thought you could spend the night, then I would take you home in the morning."

"What about your parents?"

"They live in the main house. We are totally alone back here," Silas told Luka, reaching over to rub Luka's crotch, again, in order to change his focus.

As Luka looked around and thought about how isolated they were, Silas did what he could to direct Luka's blood flow to the southern region of his body. Silas leaned over and kissed Luka's neck. As Luka's entire body began to tingle, he relaxed and decided he wasn't in danger.

Luka pushed Silas back, in order to take control of the situation. "Oh yeah, I'm okay with it. Let's go inside," Luka said, leaning over and hooking his hand behind Silas' neck.

Luka pulled Silas to him and passionately kissed Silas as his shaft became engorged and became tight under his denim. When they pulled back, they gazed into each others eyes, before exiting the vehicle and heading inside. Silas interlocked his fingers with Luka and led him into the bedroom of the cabin. They sat down next to each other on one edge of the bed. Luka placed his hand on Silas' knee and slowly slid his hand up to his groin. As Luka rubbed his hand back and forth along Silas' erection, Silas leaned over and kissed Luka's neck.

As his engorged member pressed up against his zipper, wanting to be released, Silas slung his leg around Luka's knees and straddled him. Silas removed his own shirt first, then Luka's shirt. As he did so, he writhed his hips back and forth, rubbing his erection against Luka's. As his excitement grew, Silas became more and more aggressive.

Luka moaned with pleasure as Silas pressed his hand against Luka's throat and forced him to lay back on the bed. Silas fumbled with unbuttoning Luka's pants, pulled the zipper down, then stood in front of

Luka and grabbed ahold of the waistband, yanking them down to Luka's ankles.

As soon as Luka was completely naked, Silas grasped Luka around his hips and flipped Luka over onto his stomach. Silas then fiddled with the button and zipper of his own pants with one hand, while pressing his other hand against the middle of Luka's back.

After he had removed his own trousers, Silas again grabbed Luka by his hips and positioned Luka up on his hands and knees. Silas climbed up on the bed on his knees behind Luka, pulling Luka's bottom against his erection, slipping his shaft up and down between Luka's cheeks.

As Silas positioned the tip of his penis against Luka's opening, Luka moaned with anticipation. Silas grabbed Luka's hips, then shoved himself into Luka. Once they were in the midst of coitus, Luka kept trying to reach around in order to touch Silas. Silas wanted all control of the situation, so he leaned forward and pressed Luka's face into the mattress.

Luka kept trying to turn his head to the side, as he

felt as though he was suffocating being held down to the mattress. Once he was able to get out from under Silas' hand, he lifted his head up and gasped for air.

Luka continued to writhe in rhythm together with Silas, unaware that Silas had reached under one of the pillows and grabbed the rope he had staged before hand. With a quick motion, as Luka continued to take deep breaths, Silas flung the rope over Luka's head and wrapped it around his neck. Silas crossed over the two ends of the rope and pulled hard as he began to strangle Luka.

Luka reached up and frantically grabbed at the garrote stifling his oxygen, struggled to breathe, as Silas continued thrusting into him. Just as Luka's body went limp and he stopped struggling, Silas tightened his grip on the rope, pulled harder and climaxed. He heard the bones in his victim's neck snap before he let go of the rope.

Silas collapsed onto the bed and cuddled with Luka's dead body until he recovered from the trembling pleasured sensation of his orgasm. He felt as though he was having an out of body experience. It was as if he was actually floating above and peering down at the two bodies curled together on the center of the bed.

Silas' hands were chafed and bloody from having the rope hooked around his thumbs and pulling tight with his palms. He leaned up on his elbow and looked down at his victim. The skin around Luka's neck had been rubbed raw and the white rope was stained red.

As he ran his finger along the rope burn on his victim, Silas turned Luka's head in order to look into his eyes. Luka had died with his eyes wide open and Silas admired the petechial hemorrhaging that was covering the sclera.

Once he had recovered and was ready to get up, he snapped to the realization that he was going to have to get rid of the body. Silas stood up, dressed into Luka's clothing and went out into a heavily wooded area on the property behind the cabin.

He grabbed a shovel that he had placed against a tree in preparation for that moment and dug a grave before going back to the cabin to retrieve his victim. He slung Luka's naked body over his shoulder and carried it outside. Stepping up next to the hole, Silas whipped the body off his shoulder and tossed it down into the grave. Silas felt disconnected from the intimate activity he had engaged in with this once lively person.

Without hesitation, he reached for the shovel and replaced the dirt to the earth, completely covering the body and filling in the hole. After patting the dirt with the spade of the shovel, Silas stepped over the grave in order to return to the cabin to clean up and change back into his own clothes.

Silas walked into the kitchen area, grabbed a trash bag out from under the sink and took it into the bedroom. As he pealed off the dirty clothes, he stuffed them into the trash bag, then headed in to shower in the cabin bathroom.

Once he was dressed in his own clothing, he stood in front of the full length mirror and took a deep satisfying breath. He headed back into the bedroom and stripped off the sheets and blankets from the bed, stuffing them into the trash bag as well. Silas walked to the closet and retrieved a clean set of sheets and a new blanket, making the bed perfectly, in order to give the appearance that nothing had occurred there. Before he headed back to his parents' house, Silas picked up the trash bag containing his victim's clothing and the bed sheets, then stuffed in Luka's shoes which were left outside the front door.

Heading out to his vehicle, Silas tossed the bag into the trunk before sliding in behind the wheel. He drove back to the main house and went straight to his room for the night. The next day he tossed the bag of his victim's items in the burn pit on the property and never gave it a second thought; that was until he needed to find another victim.

When Silas joined his family for breakfast the next morning, he was in a great mood. Neither his parents, nor his little sister had any idea of what he had done the night before. No one asked about the wounds on his hands, they were just glad to see he was happy again. He had been having those feelings since he had hit puberty, but he wasn't able to complete the act. Luckily, with Luka, he had decided to use the rope, because the first few times, when he had tried manual strangulation, his victims were able to get out from under his grasp.

After his first successful kill with Luka, he continued claiming unsuspecting men twice a year. He perfected his garrote, in order to avoid the rope burns on his hands.

When he graduated from high school, Silas went on to college in an accounting program. He graduated at the top of his class and managed to start his own accounting firm and generally worked from home. His victim count never waned through college, nor when he opened his own accounting firm.

His parents had allowed him to move into the cabin on their property until he had saved enough money to move out on his own. The privacy of the cabin assisted in his bi-yearly activity and he needed to be sure that his own home gave him the same kind of privacy.

TWO

By the time he made it to the age of twenty eight, Silas began looking into purchasing his own home. He wanted the house to be basically solitary, but with a few neighbors just so he could seem normal. When he was looking through the listings, there was one house that called out to him. It was at the end of a cul-de-sac and only had three other homes near it.

At the end of the cul-de-sac, in the back of the neighborhood, there were four isolated homes. Those homes were surrounded by a wooded area, secluded from the rest of the neighborhood. When one of those homes went up for sale, he put in an offer as an anonymous buyer. Who could have known what kind of domino effect that would create?

He put the offer on the house based on the photos he saw online. When he was contacted by the real estate agent and informed the seller had accepted his offer, he immediately began packing as well as stalking his new victim.

Silas wanted to christen his new home with a new target. He managed to convince the real estate agent and the seller of the home to allow him to move in within fourteen days instead of thirty. He was overly excited and was ready to bring home the man he had been vetting.

When he turned into the neighborhood, the entrance had a brick sign separating the in and out lanes surrounded by beautiful landscaping. As he drove down the main road, he called the realtor in order to get an idea of how the neighborhood was set up.

"Drive straight down the main road to the end. There are side streets that branch off the main road, but your house is past all that in the back," the realtor told Silas.

"I see that each side road has its own section name and entrance. What is down those side roads?" Silas asked.

"The entrances to each section are about twenty yards to a stop sign. There is a house directly across the street from the stop sign which gives the option to turn either left or right. Either direction circles back around to the entrance of the section and there are houses on both sides of the street all the way around the circle. Basically, the entire neighborhood is set up as one main road, with a bunch of no outlet roads that all create their own section."

"What about a homeowners association?"

"Due to the set up of the neighborhood, there is no HOA. The homeowners in each section are to come to an agreement on how they would like their sections to appear. There are, however, a few homeowners in each section who feel the need to police the others, but in general, everyone follows the rules of their sections."

As Silas drove around the neighborhood, he was disappointed to see how close together the houses were and the fact that the front yards were basically nonexistent. Silas made his way to the back of the neighborhood where his new home was located, hoping for more space between him and his neighbors.

In some sections, all of the homeowners really cared about the appearance of their lawns. They were perfectly maintained and lush. In other sections, none of the homeowners cared about appearances. The flower beds had weeds growing out of them and the lawns were overgrown. In those sections, there were cars parked up and down the streets.

"Each section basically has its own reputation and the residents only socialized with their own section, so you won't have to worry about going to meetings with random neighbors, just the few that live near you," the realtor continued.

At the end of the main road was section twenty five, Islander. It was a no outlet road with a cul-de-sac at the end. The four homes in that section were perfectly isolated while still maintaining the appearance of normalcy that Silas needed. Luckily, those homes were built on a couple acres of land each, rather than a quarter of an acre like the rest of the homes in the neighborhood.

As he pulled up to the first house to his right, he parked in the driveway and admired his new home. It was built back in the nineteen fifties and seemed to have its original yellow and white paint on the outside. It was a ranch style, single story home with a detached garage that was most likely added in the nineties. The realtor was waiting for him on the driveway, in order to pass him the keys.

"So, what do you know about the other neighbors here?" Silas asked, as he hung up his phone and walked up to his realtor.

"Not much. I know each house has a family. Mom, dad and some kids. I don't know how many kids each family has, but I know each one of them has kids," the realtor told him.

"I hope they don't let their kids come out here, screaming in the street. I work from home and really value my privacy."

"Hopefully your new home is a peaceful halidom for you and your neighbors are pleasant."

As the realtor left Silas, he began retrieving some of his belongings from the trunk of his car. A couple of the neighbors had emerged from their homes and walked up. At first they just stood there watching him as he stacked up a few things on the driveway.

"Hello there, new neighbor," a woman said from behind him.

Silas turned around to see two women standing near the bottom of his driveway, just at the opening to the sidewalk. He could tell that they hadn't picked up on his sexual orientation due to the flirtatious waves and their posture.

"Well, hello ladies," he said. "What can I do for you?"

"We just wanted to introduce ourselves and welcome you to the island. I'm Cybil and this is Karen. I live right next to you and Karen lives across the street. Michelle lives in the house between us, but she has young children so she hardly ever comes out if her husband isn't home."

Cybil was probably in her mid-forties. She had her chocolate brown hair cut short that was obviously done for convenience. As she spoke, she continuously ran her fingers through her chin length bob as if she were trying to style it on the spot. Her make-up appeared to be thrown on in haste due to the very visible foundation line all the way around her hairline as well as along her jawline.

Karen on the other hand was probably in her late-forties to early-fifties. Her hair was longer on top and very short on the sides and back. She had her hair styled and had so much hair spray in her hair, even a category five hurricane couldn't move it out of place. Her make-up was perfect as if she were overcompensating for her cheating husband.

Silas was sure he would meet Michelle soon, but imagined her to be in her late-twenties to early thirties, long disheveled hair pulled up in a loose bun and no make-up. Both Cybil and Karen were wearing shorts, ensuring to cover their thighs down to their knees; most likely trying to cover the cellulite they had accumulated from having children and eating too many snack foods. Their shirts, on the other hand, were low cut and revealed more cleavage than what Silas was comfortable with.

He introduced himself, smiling flirtatiously, "I'm Silas and I'm happy to be here. This is my first home and I hope I can be a good neighbor."

The ladies giggled like a couple of high school girls talking to their crush and stepped up closer to him. Silas knew he had this kind of effect on women, even though his shorts were mid-thigh - exposing all of his leg muscles - and he had cut the sleeves and the midriff off his shirt. He was young and worked out a lot. In order to have the strength to snap the neck of his victims and to make sure to attract the men he wanted to pick up, he needed to take pride in his appearance.

"Did you need any help with anything?" Karen asked, stroking his bicep with her finger.

"No, I think I can manage. The moving truck should be here soon, so I will have four more guys to help. I appreciate your offer," Silas said, respectfully.

"Well, if you need anything, and I mean anything, you know where to find us," Cybil said, before turning to walk away.

Silas watched as the two ladies walked away giggling and looking back to catch another glimpse of him before heading into Cybil's house. Closing the trunk to his car, he shook his head as he picked up the three boxes he had stacked up on the driveway before heading toward his front door.

As soon as he had opened the door, the moving truck pulled up. The four guys in the truck were friends of Silas that he had met at the gym a few years back. They ran a moving company and agreed to help.

Derik was of Indigenous descent and wore his long hair in a pony tail if he was working or working out. He was twenty eight and enjoyed any time he was able to spend with Silas. Since Silas always gave off the perception that he was happy being able to live the single life, Derik attempted to mirror that perception, but the friend group knew he had feelings for Silas.

Barry was in his thirties and had been dating the same guy for ten years. They thought about getting married, but didn't know if they wanted to combine everything they owned. They still lived in separate apartments, but spent all their time together. They alternated weeks that they spent at each other's place and even worked together.

Greg was Barry's boyfriend. He seemed to like their arrangement, but sometimes Silas felt like he wanted more out of the relationship. Barry looked like Terry Crews and was mistaken for him all the time. Greg looked more like John Cena, but like a dad version - cargo shorts and a tucked in crew shirt.

Frankie was the effeminate one. He always wore shirts that were two sizes too small, so they were tight around his slender frame and showed off his midriff, along with cutoff denim shorts that he cut himself. He had a fanny pack around his waist due to the fact that his shorts were too tight around his rock hard ass and he needed a place to put his wallet and his lip gloss.

Silas seemed to make friends easily, which assisted in his attempt to appear as normal as possible. It helped that he was able to blend in no matter where he went, so after eleven years of claiming two victims per year he was still a free man. He was also able to keep his extracurricular activities a secret from his friends, because he knew they would turn him in.

"Hey Silas, where is this stuff going?" Derik asked, climbing out from behind the wheel of the moving truck.

"Just bring it inside and stack the boxes in the dining room. As for the large furniture, I'll direct you to the room it needs to go in," Silas informed, as Barry and Greg opened the back of the truck.

"You got it, beef cake," Frankie said, slipping on a pair of gloves that were more for fashion reasons rather than for moving furniture.

As the guys brought in the furniture, Cybil and Karen brought out lawn chairs and placed them on Cybil's driveway to watch. They were holding drinks and sipping on straws with a pitcher of, what Silas assumed was, margaritas sitting on the driveway between them.

The ladies waved at the strong men anytime they looked over in their direction, then giggled when the men waved back. Eventually a woman, whom Silas assumed was Michelle, appeared from the house next to Cybil and joined the other ladies. She had a baby monitor in her hand and would put it up to her ear every-so-often. Her appearance was exactly as Silas had imagined.

"You have some very nice neighbors, Silas," Greg said.

"Unfortunately, they seem like they would be very disappointed to find out that their new neighbor is a gay man," Silas informed them.

"Maybe I should go over there and say hi," Frankie said, bouncing on his toes.

"How about we finish moving me in first, before we freak out the neighbors. Besides, they will find out the first time I bring someone home," Silas said, with the biggest smile on his face.

Once the truck was empty, Silas and his friends separated the boxes into the rooms to which they belonged. As everything was organized in a way to make it easier for Silas to unpack, the other four guys headed out in order to take the truck back to the lot where they parked it.

"How about we meet up for dinner and drinks later," Frankie asked, as they stood on the driveway of Silas' house.

"As long as you promise not to get shit faced," Silas replied.

"Oh honey, you know I always get shit faced when I drink. It gives the illusion that I'm easy," Frankie said, gyrating his hips.

"That's no illusion, you *are* easy," Derik said, laughing.

"That's true," Frankie said, flirtatiously.

"Well, I'm in," Derik said.

"Me too," Silas agreed.

"I guess we could participate," Barry said, as Greg nodded.

The guys left and Silas returned inside his new home. After the kitchen was unpacked and organized, Silas broke down the boxes, as he thought about his next kill. He decided he would meet the other guys for dinner and drinks, then head out to meet up with his target.

Three

Silas made sure to drink less than his friends to ensure that he was sober when he approached his victim later that night. Barry and Greg summoned a ride share driver to get home safely, while Derik and Frankie said they were going to walk.

"You are twenty-five miles from either of your

homes. How about I give you two a ride to make sure you get home without getting lost?" Silas suggested.

"Fuck, twenty-five miles is far," Derik said, agreeing to ride with Silas.

"I want to go to a bar and maybe get some bear to take me home," Frankie said, stumbling down the sidewalk.

"Get in the fucking car, drunky," Derik yelled down the street at Frankie.

"Come on buddy, I'll take you home," Silas told Frankie, placing his arm over his drunk friend's shoulders and leading him over to his car.

"But you're not a bear, sir," Frankie said, putting his hand up Silas' shirt and rubbing his bare chest. "I like my men hairy with a little jiggle in the middle."

"Oh, I know. I have seen the guys you date. Now, if you don't mind, please get in the car so we can go," Silas told him, directing Frankie toward his car.

"Fine, but you owe me," Frankie said, tapping Silas on his chest with his fingertips and climbing in the backseat with Derik, laying his head on Derik's lap.

"Don't get fresh with me, I might expect more if you do," Derik told Frankie, looking down at him.

"We tried that, honey and it didn't work. I will just go home and diddle to porn," Frankie said, sitting up as Silas climbed into the driver's seat.

"Oh god Frankie, why do you have to call it diddling?" Derik asked.

"That's what my mom called it when she caught me with my first Bear Magazine," Frankie said, wiggling his eyebrows.

"Okay, we are no longer talking about your diddle. I have other things I would like to think about," Silas said.

"Did you want to talk about *your* diddle?" Frankie asked, leaning forward between the front seats.

"How about we just focus on getting you home," Derik said, placing his hand on Frankie's shoulder and pulling him back into the seat.

"Fine, I have a nail appointment tomorrow anyway and I need my beauty sleep," Frankie said, holding his right hand out as if to admire his nails.

"Please don't get those fake nails again. You can't

lift boxes and furniture with those things and they make you act like a queen," Derik said, rubbing his forehead.

"No, it's nothing like that. I'm just getting a clear coat put on along with a trim. Plus, I love it when they do my feet. I get a massage and everything," Frankie informed. "Maybe you should come with me, Derik. It could help you relax. You seem a little tense."

"Nothing a little diddle won't fix," Silas said, laughing.

"Oh really? How about I diddle you and you diddle me?" Derik asked, reaching up and rubbing Silas' arm.

"Damn, how long has it been for you, Derik? If you are willing to diddle with Silas, it has to have been a long time," Frankie said.

"Gee, thanks Frankie. Good to know that I'm a last resort diddle," Silas said.

"That's not what I meant. It's just, you never have relationships. You have only had one-night-stands and that's the end of it. Plus, we all know that you have a thing for Derik anyway," Frankie tried to save his ass and change the focus on to someone else.

"I have some very specific sexual needs and some guys just can't hang for more than one night. As for the Derik comment, I'm not in a place in my life right now to have a relationship and he deserves that," Silas defended, without giving away too much.

"Wow, so your diddle is that big?" Frankie said, again leaning up between the front seats.

"Oh, look at that Frankie. We are at your house," Silas said, as he pulled up in front of the duplex that Frankie lived in, feeling relieved.

"Okay guys, see ya later," Frankie said, exiting the vehicle.

Derik moved from the back seat to the passenger seat, as Silas watched Frankie unlock and open his front door. Derik buckled his seatbelt and Silas pulled away from the curb.

"We have to stop getting drunk with him," Derik said.

"I agree with that. I'm surprised he didn't try to grab my dick," Silas admitted.

"So, seriously. You want to go back to my place,

or yours?" Derik said, gently stroking Silas' cheek.

"I'm sorry Derik. I like having you as a friend and I don't want to do anything to jeopardize our friendship," Silas said, reaching up and turning his head in order to kiss the palm of Derik's hand.

Derik pulled his hand back and placed it in his lap. "I understand. I just feel like we could work together. I really like you."

"And I like you. It's just...," Silas stopped, thinking he might say too much.

"Just what? I'm not good looking enough for you?"

"That is not it at all. I'm just not ready for a serious relationship and you deserve someone who is willing to devote all of themselves to you. But like I told Frankie, I have some very specific sexual needs."

"Oh god. You're not straight, are you?" Derik said, with a disgusted look on his face.

"Gross, no. What I mean is, there are certain things I like and I feel more comfortable acting on those things when I know I don't have to see the guy ever again," Silas explained.

"And you aren't afraid to run into the guy at any time afterward?"

"Not at all. I always pick them up from a place I have never been before and that I don't ever plan on returning to."

"But what if you end up actually liking the guy and decide you want to see him again?"

"I guess I will find out when that day comes," Silas said, as he pulled up to the home that Derik shared with three female roommates.

"Well, I will always be around when you are ready for a real relationship," Derik told him, leaning over and passionately kissing Silas, right on the mouth.

Silas gave in and kissed him back. It only lasted a few seconds, but both men were fully aroused. Derik pulled back from the kiss and looked deeply into Silas' eyes before exiting the vehicle and walking up to his front door.

Silas watched Derik enter the home and lightly touched his fingertips to his lips. He had been caught off guard. He didn't know if he wanted to go inside and ravage Derik, or continue on with his plan for the evening. He rubbed his crotch, trying to tame his sexual urge, then decided he needed to release during a kill and not give in to Derik.

Four

Silas drove for over an hour into a small town where he had been stalking his next victim. He knew the man he had chosen would be at a specific bar in town.

As he pulled into the parking area to the bar, Silas went over his plan in his head. Once he was comfortable with the plan and was sure it would work, he exited his vehicle and headed inside the bar.

Once inside the front doors, Silas familiarized himself with the layout - just in case something went wrong and he wanted to make a quick getaway. There were five billiard tables, with at least four men at each, spaced throughout the open area. In a far right corner, there was a sign on a door indicating the restroom. Ten feet from the front door was a bar top that sat approximately twenty people. Lucky for Silas, only three people occupied the seats at the bar and everyone else was grouped around the billiard tables.

Silas moved through the crowd and planted himself on one of the barstools closest to the bathroom. He began looking around at each patron, carefully studying their facial features, when the bartender approached him from the other side of the bar.

"What can I get fer ya, buddy?" the bartender inquired, speaking with a thick southern accent.

"Gin martini, dry," Silas told him, without turning to look at him.

"You got it," the bartender said, beginning to mix

the drink.

When his drink was placed on the bar in front of him, Silas had spotted his target sitting alone at a small table meant for two, tucked back in a corner, just outside the bathroom door. He turned around, gave the bartender a ten dollar bill, then swiveled back in his chair hoping to make eye contact with his chosen.

Twenty minutes and two more drinks later, the man finally looked up toward the bar top. Silas wasn't sure if he was looking at him, or if he was trying to get the bartender's attention for another beer. Silas held his martini glass up and nodded his head, as if to say hello from afar. The man looked around at the few other patrons in his vicinity, then realized Silas was acknowledging him.

He turned back to face Silas, smiled and returned the gesture. Silas tilted his head, summoning his victim to him. As his plan began to take form, the man stood and made his way to the bar top, stopping in front of Silas.

"I don't think I have ever seen you in here before,"

the man told Silas.

"I'm just passing through and decided to stop in for a few drinks and a little company," Silas informed him. "I'm Silas, by the way."

"I'm Wesley," he said, presenting his hand to Silas.

"Have a seat," Silas told him, grabbing his hand and guiding him toward the barstool next to him.

Wesley climbed up onto the barstool next to Silas, then tapped the rim of his pint glass with his finger to get the attention of the bartender. The bartender gave both of them refills on their drinks.

"So Wesley, what do you do for a living?" Silas asked.

"I'm a mobile mechanic. What about you?" Wesley replied.

"I'm an accountant."

"Well, that's impressive. I bet you live in a big fancy house in the middle of the big city."

"Actually, I live in a modest home in the back of a neighborhood in the suburbs."

"Modest huh? What is that code for, mansion?"

"It's hardly a mansion. It's a single story, three thousand square foot home. As a matter of fact, I just moved in and was looking to take someone home with me, in order to christen my new house. Would you be interested?" Silas asked, placing his hand on Wesley's thigh.

"Oh, so it's like that," Wesley said, placing his hand on top of Silas' hand and sliding it up a little higher on his leg. "Well, if that's what you are looking for, what kind of car do you drive?"

"Well, my car is a different story. My car helps me pick up dates."

Silas slid his hand up further until he was rubbing Wesley's crotch. He could feel the arousal in his target, which in turn aroused him. Wesley downed his beer, stood up off the barstool and placed his hand between Silas' legs, cupping his manhood.

"Pay the bill and pick me up outside," Wesley whispered in his ear before licking his lobe.

Wesley headed toward the bathroom, as Silas watched him walk away. He placed a fifty dollar bill down on the bar before heading out to his car. As Silas waited for Wesley to emerge from the bar, he imagined what shade of grey his victim's skin would turn within the first thirty minutes after death.

After a couple of minutes, Wesley appeared and Silas felt the anticipation of the remainder of the evening's events. Silas raised his arm up over his head and waved in order to get Wesley's attention. As his target headed toward him, Silas opened the driver's side door and slid in behind the wheel, pushing the button to start up his car. Wesley hastily approached the vehicle, opened the passenger door and joined Silas in the front seat.

As soon as both doors were closed, Silas placed his hand on the back of Wesley's neck and pulled the unsuspecting victim's face to his. Silas pressed his lips against Wesley's and made sure that his target was so aroused that he would not question the distance to his home.

When Silas pulled out of the kiss, Wesley had unzipped his pants and was beginning to pleasure himself in the car. Silas placed his hand over Wesley's exposed genitals and leaned over to whisper in his ear.

"Just wait until we get to my house. I promise it will be worth it," Silas said, tracing the entire shape of Wesley's ear with his tongue.

"I don't know if I can wait," Wesley pleaded. "You want to just pull over down a dark road and climb into the back seat?"

"Please, I promise. The back seat is too cramped and at my house, I can twist you into so many different positions, you won't be able to catch your breath," Silas told him.

Wesley took a deep breath before stuffing his erection down into his fly, zipping his pants back up and just rubbed himself through the denim. Silas shifted the car into reverse, backed out of the parking space, then shifted into drive and pulled out of the parking area.

He drove as quickly as he could to try to make it back to his house sooner than the hour and a half it took him to arrive at the bar. Wesley continued to rub himself through his pants and moan loudly.

Fifteen minutes into the drive, Wesley reached over and began rubbing Silas's crotch through his pants. As his excitement grew, Silas pressed the gas pedal and sped up. Now *he* was having trouble waiting.

As he swung his car up into his driveway, Silas managed to make an hour and a half drive in forty minutes. He shifted into park, then grabbed Wesley's wrist.

"Once we get inside, we can finish this up," Silas told him.

Wesley flung the door open and climbed out of the car as Silas pressed the button to turn his car off and exited the vehicle as well. Before he had closed the driver's door, Wesley had already made his way around the car and pressed his body against Silas as they kissed.

"Silas, is that you?" Cybil's voice echoed from her driveway next door.

"Yes Cybil, it's me," Silas answered, as soon as Wesley pulled back from the kiss.

"Who is that with you?" Cybil pried.

"Oh hello. I'm-," Wesley started, but Silas cut him off.

"He's my date. I hope I didn't disturb you," Silas said.

"He? Like a man? You're gay?" Cybil nearly choked on her words.

"Yes ma'am. Is that a problem?" Silas asked.

Cybil didn't answer. She just scoffed, then ran to Karen's house and pounded on her front door. Silas hooked his elbow with Wesley's and led him up to his front door. As soon as the door was open, Silas reached for the button of Wesley's pants.

"Now, let's get our clothes off and do what we came here to do," Silas said, before closing the door.

Five

The next morning, Silas woke up next to Wesley's dead body. The rope had been pulled so tight around his neck, Wesley had almost been decapitated. His spine and trachea were exposed and the bed sheet was stained with blood around his head. His skin was almost a silver coloring with a blueish tint to his lips.

Silas lightly kissed his victim on the forehead before sitting up on the edge of his bed and placing his feet on the floor. He wiggled his toes and stretched his arms up over his head, feeling the realignment of his facet joints, along with the release of air within the synovial fluid of his shoulders and elbows.

Before getting rid of the body, Silas headed into the bathroom to shower. Once he was dressed and ready for the day, he pulled the fitted sheet up from each corner, placed the pillows on the floor and, using the bedding, slid Wesley's body off his bed and dropped it to the floor.

He headed out to the kitchen to get his roll of plastic sheeting to wrap up the body, when he heard someone knocking on his front door. Silas sighed, then walked over to find out who had disturbed his morning.

"Hello ladies," Silas said, after opening the door.

Cybil and Karen were standing shoulder to shoulder, while Michelle was peeking from behind them.

"We need to talk," Karen said, tapping her foot on the doorstep.

"Can this wait until after I've had breakfast?" Silas requested.

"We could always come in and just talk to you now," Cybil suggested, as her and Karen stepped forward as if they were going to try and force their way in.

"Are you just wanting to see how gay my house is?" Silas asked, with a hint of sarcasm in his voice.

"We just want to keep our kids safe," Michelle said, from behind the other two ladies.

"How is me being a part of the LGBTQ community unsafe for your children?" Silas asked.

"Cybil and I have children that are old enough to understand that boys shouldn't kiss boys. It's immoral and I don't want your influence to rub off onto my ten year old son, as well as Cybil's son," Karen told him, wagging her finger in his face.

"Are y'all just afraid that if your boys see me and my friends prancing around and kissing each other out on my driveway, that your two boys may want to kiss each other?" Silas questioned, squinting his eyes and furrowing his brow.

"Your extra curricular activities are absolutely unsavory and you're not welcome here," Cybil said, poking his chest with her stubby finger.

"Look, I'm not sure who you ladies think I am, but I can assure you that I am not going to do anything unsavory in front of your children. Now, if we are done here, I would really like to have my coffee and breakfast alone," Silas said, before closing the door in their faces.

After making sure to lock the door, he headed back toward his kitchen to complete the task he was interrupted from. Reaching under the kitchen sink, Silas retrieved the roll of black plastic sheeting and headed back into his bedroom.

Unrolling the plastic along the floor at the foot of his bed, Silas cut the roll once he had enough to conceal the body. He set the rest of the plastic aside, then lifted the dead body of his victim up off the floor and placed it in the center of the plastic. He wrapped up the body from head to toe, placing electrical tape around the neck, the waist, - holding the arms down against the torso - and the ankles to ensure the plastic didn't unravel. Silas then slung the body over his shoulder and headed out his back door toward his detached garage.

He placed the body on the floor of the garage, left and locked the door, heading back into his house for breakfast. There was no way in hell he wanted to talk to his neighbors until he had, at least, his first cup of coffee.

Silas scrambled a couple of eggs and placed two pieces of bread in the toaster while his coffee brewed. He turned his television on to the news, as he sat down to relax and eat.

"Another woman's body was discovered early this morning. Police believe foul play was involved and there is a connection to the eight other bodies that have been found over the past couple of years. Law enforcement still has no leads on who the killer might be, but with evidence mounting, they are confident they are closing in on the suspect. Stay tuned to news eight for continuing coverage," the news anchor said.

"That killer is an idiot. Leaving those bodies out in the open," Silas said, as he stuffed the last bite of toast into his mouth.

Once he had finished his morning meal, he placed his breakfast dishes into the sink, poured himself a second cup of coffee and headed out his front door.

The three ladies had set up four chairs on Cybil's driveway, all facing Silas' house. As Silas wandered over to join them, the women maneuvered the chairs into a circle. After he sat down, Karen decided to speak first.

"Cybil says she saw you kissing a man on your driveway last night," Karen said, leaning forward.

"Does that make you ladies uncomfortable?" Silas inquired.

"We just think *that* kind of behavior in public is inappropriate. If you could please keep your private life a little more…private, that would be appreciated," Karen said.

"Well, I could technically say the same to you. Karen, I have seen you chase your husband out of the house, begging him for a kiss before he leaves for work. As for you, Cybil, the next time you and your husband want to have a little 'private time' while your kids are watching a movie in another room, maybe you should close your curtains. I do not want to be subjected to your heterosexuality," Silas told them, smirking.

"If you can't keep your unsavory activities confined to the inside of your house, we may have to vote you out of the section. Back here in the Islander Section, we like to focus on family values," Michelle stated.

"Well, there is one thing I know, you can't kick me out of my home for being gay," Silas said, standing. "If you don't like it, *you* can always move."

"We are the homeowner's association of this section. Each section has their own HOA and we have the power to vote you out of the section," Karen said, standing as well and again wagging her finger in Silas' face.

"I doubt that. I specifically made sure with the real estate agent that there was no HOA. So, go back to your boring lives," he told them.

Silas took the final gulp of his coffee and walked back to his house. He knew there where shitty people in the world, but after they sat and watched him and his buddies when they unloaded the moving truck, he figured they would be a little more accepting.

He walked into his house and made sure to dead-bolt his front door. Silas headed toward the kitchen and placed his coffee mug into the sink. For a few moments he debated whether or not to wash his morning dishes, or just go straight out to bury Wesley's body.

Realizing he could be spotted in the daylight engaging in suspicious behavior, Silas decided that it would probably be safer to wait until the middle of the night before he started digging a hole. Especially a grave sized hole.

Once his dishes were washed and put away, Silas picked up his phone and called Derik to make sure he was okay with the previous day's events and ask him for a favor.

"Don't worry about it. I was drunk," Derik told Silas.

"I'm so glad we are okay. Now, I have a favor to ask," Silas told him. "Is there anyway you could get me about ten potted tulips? I'm looking at putting in a flower bed in my backyard and thought I would start with tulips."

"Absolutely, that is no problem. When do you need them by?"

"Is tomorrow morning too soon?"

"Not at all. If you want, I can get them to you this afternoon and help you dig the new flower bed."

"Actually, I plan on pissing off my homophobic neighbors by digging it up at two in the morning and making as much noise as possible," Silas said, laughing.

"Your new neighbors are homophobic? They seemed so nice when we were helping you move in," Derik said.

"I was spotted with my date last night and this morning they made it pretty clear they do not approve of my lifestyle."

"Who knew you would be the one to move into a home with bigoted bitches as neighbors?"

"Why just me? Any one of us could end up in this situation."

"You are just such a likable guy."

"Oh yeah, that's a reason for close minded bitches to look past my gayness. Maybe I should use that the next time they tell me that my lifestyle is not something they want around their children, '*but I'm a nice guy*'," Silas said, sarcastically.

"I'm just saying. Well, I'll see you in the morning," Derik said, before disconnecting the call.

After hanging up the phone, Silas did a little work for his clients, waiting for his time to dispose of his victim. Later that night, around ten, Silas decided to sit on his driveway, shirtless and with a cooler full of beer, watching the neighbor's houses. He watched and waited for them to turn off all the lights in their houses to signify they had gone to bed.

Once all three homes were dark and quiet, Silas went out to his detached garage and retrieved the body. He grabbed a camping lantern on his way out, carrying the body out to the far end of his yard and laying it down up against the fence. Lighting the lantern, he returned to the garage to retrieve a shovel.

As he dug the grave, he made sure it wasn't a perfect rectangle. He gave one long side a half circle as an appealing shape for a tulip garden. At about four feet down, Silas stopped and jammed the spade end of the shovel into the pile of dirt he made. He walked around and crouched down next to the body. Scooping his arms underneath, he shoved it into the grave.

Silas placed his elbow on the end of the shovel and admired his work. He heard a noise coming from Cybil's house, then quickly filled in the hole. Making sure the dirt was pliable for planting.

Six

Over the next few weeks, one by one, each one of the other three homes went up for sale. They each had the same real estate agent, Karen's husband. Silas made sure to call Derik, Frankie, Barry and Greg to come over to hang out when they had their scheduled open houses, just to upset them.

"Hi. Don't mind us. We are just a group of gay men who regularly engage in gay activities on the front lawn. I hope you are okay with that," Frankie would call out to potential buyers.

"Would you stop that," Barry told Frankie.

"Why? If we plan to hang out here on a regular basis, I want to make sure that the new owners aren't total homophobic twats like the bitches living there now," Frankie defended his actions.

"I don't mind. These women were inappropriate when they approached me about my date. What business is it of theirs of my sexual orientation? Keep going Frankie. Make sure the new buyers aren't bigots," Silas told him.

Day after day, the five of them would set up post on Silas' driveway and Frankie would cat call the men who would stop by to view the homes. Once Barry was on board with Frankie making the potential buyers uncomfortable, they would all laugh.

After weeks of the guys sitting on Silas' driveway, finally the real estate agent posted a sold sign to the first house to sell; Karen's house, across the street.

Karen and her family had moved out two weeks after the sold sign went up.

A moving truck pulled up the following week. The new homeowner arrived shortly after the truck, unlocked the front door and allowed the movers to take his furniture inside before walking over and introducing himself to Silas and his friends.

"Hello neighbor. I'm Zayn Miller," the new neighbor said, extending his hand to the group.

Zayn Miller stood at approximately six feet, two inches and about two hundred fifty pounds. He was wearing athletic shorts and a tank undershirt. His brown hair was long on top, but cut short on the sides.

"I'm Silas Graham. I live in this house. These are my friends. That's Barry, Greg, Derik and Frankie. Maybe we could all hang out some time. We get together every weekend and have guy time," Silas told him.

"Hello sir," Frankie said, approaching Zayn, presenting his hand as though he was expecting Zayn to kiss his knuckles.

Zayn gently held Frankie's fingers with one hand,

placing his other hand over the back of Frankie's and made eye contact with him, smiling. Frankie giggled and pranced back to his chair, as Zayn moved on and shook hands with each of the other guys. Silas went into his garage, pulled out another chair and Zayn joined them.

While the movers emptied their truck across the street, Zayn told the guys about his background and how he came to live across the street from Silas.

"My mother was and still is, totally over protective. My father on the other hand became violently abusive when he drank. I have always been a relaxed and laid back person. I never shared my home life with anyone growing up. Whenever my father would beat on my mother, she would sleep in my room, which was more often than not. By the time I was ten, my mother had put bunk beds in my room," Zayn started.

What he didn't share with his new neighbors was that the subsequent days after his father would beat on his mother, Zayn would capture and torture small wild animals; rabbits, squirrels, raccoons and opossums.

He vowed that one day his father would become his first human victim. That day came when he was seventeen.

"One day, in my late teens, my father had beaten my mother so severely, she was barely alive by the time I got her to the hospital. My father was arrested, but released a couple weeks later with only five years of probation. My mother blamed herself for him not receiving any jail time. It was due to the fact that she had never reported any of the abuse, so his attorney was able to get him probation as an isolated incident," Zayn continued.

When his father returned to the house after being released, Zayn was there waiting for him. He refused to allow his father to hurt his mother anymore, so he killed him before she was released from the hospital.

He was sitting on the sofa when his father entered the home. Laid out on the coffee table in front of Zayn, was a butcher knife, a steak knife and a machete. Once his father began insulting him, Zayn lurched forward off the sofa, picked up the butcher knife first and lunged toward his father.

As the knife was plunged into his father's round gut, Zayn was back handed across the face and fell to the floor. His father grabbed the handle of the knife and pulled it out of his flesh, as Zayn scrambled to his feet. Zayn picked up the steak knife and went after his father again.

With several quick motions, he jabbed the knife into his father's torso until he fell to the floor. Once his father lay bleeding and gasping for air, Zayn shoved a plastic bag over his father's head and secured it with blue electrical tape around his neck.

Zayn dragged his father's body down to the basement, once he stopped breathing and left it there over night. The next morning Zayn used the machete and a hand saw in order to dismember the body. He placed the body parts in separate bags and set off for disposal.

Each bag was dumped in separate bodies of water over four different states. By the time the pieces would surface, they would just be bones. Zayn didn't tell his mother what he had done. He only told her he hadn't seen his father and that was that.

"When my mother was finally released from the hospital, I brought her home and haven't left her since. My mother became a different person once my father was gone. She was happier and more pleasant to be around. She had gained confidence and even got a job that she loved.

"After I graduated from high school, I went to college, but made sure to go to a school that was within close driving distance, so I could still live at home. I became a stock broker and have continued to live with my mother.

"A couple of months ago, she was diagnosed with breast cancer and she insisted on putting her house up for sale. She explained to me that if she were to die, I would have to pay an estate tax on the house, so it would be best if I purchased a house in my name," Zayn concluded.

As Zayn searched the internet for a secluded home, that was also in a neighborhood, he found a home in a quiet cul-de-sac. It was listed as a motivated seller home and he thought it was perfect for his mother while she went through chemotherapy. He was glad to see that the space between the homes was large enough for privacy.

Privacy was important to Zayn in order to keep his new neighbor and his friends from finding out that every three months when he takes vacation time from his job, he would stalk abusive men who beat their wives or girlfriends and murder them the same way he murdered his father.

When he felt overwhelmed, killing someone who was a complete asshole was a great stress reliever. The only misgiving he felt after he killed someone, was keeping the secret from everyone around him.

"If you ever need any help with your mother and taking her to doctor's appointments, just let me know. I work from home and I'm here most days," Silas told Zayn.

"That's really nice of you. When she's done at her chemo appointment today, I'll bring her over so you guys can meet her," Zayn said.

"How about you two come over for dinner? It will be like a welcome to the neighborhood dinner," Silas suggested.

"That would be great. Is it just going to be the three of us, or will you guys be joining us as well? I know my mom would get a kick out of knowing there is a gaggle of gay men across the street," Zayn said, chuckling.

"Oh honey, if your mom likes gay men, then we will all be here to make the two of you feel welcome," Frankie told Zayn, snapping his fingers and tossing his head back in a sassy way.

"It's settled then. Seven for dinner," Silas told him.

When the guys in the moving truck were finished unloading, Zayn told the men good bye and headed back over across the street to organize his things in his new home. Derik, Barry, Greg, Frankie and Silas continued hanging out on the drive way, discussing what they would make for dinner.

Hours later, the five men were in the kitchen of Silas' house cooking, when the doorbell rang. Frankie pranced over to answer the door.

"Hey guys, the neighbors are here," Frankie practically sang, from the front door.

The other guys emerged from the kitchen as Zayn and his mother entered the house and Frankie closed the door.

"This is my mother, Edna," Zayn introduced.

Edna was a frail old woman. She was only five feet tall and about one hundred ten pounds. The chemo treatments had caused her to lose an exorbitant amount of weight due to her aversion to food from the nausea. After her treatments she felt weak, so she was sitting in a wheel chair.

She slowly lifted her hand and each one of the men kissed her on the back of her hand as they greeted her. She giggled every time and blushed when Silas greeted her.

"It's a great pleasure to have you in my home, Edna," Silas said, as he made eye contact with her, leaning down to press his lips against the back of her hand.

"So who are the other two neighbors and why did all three of these houses go up for sale around the same time?" Edna asked, once they were seated at the table.

"They didn't like the fact that a gay man was living near their children," Silas informed her.

"Oh, pish posh. We are in the twenty-first century. People should be more accepting of alternative lifestyles. Good riddance to bad rubbish. Hopefully the other houses sell quickly so we don't have to deal with close minded human beings," Edna said.

Seven

A couple of weeks after Zayn and Edna had moved in across the street from Silas, a sold sign went up in front of Michelle's house. Within fourteen days, she had moved out of the house with the kids, leaving her husband behind to supervise the deep clean before the new owner moved in. The house was vacant for a couple of weeks before the new resident had arrived.

Silas and Zayn were sitting on Zayn's driveway when the moving truck pulled up to the house next door with a full size pickup truck close behind. There was a large magnet on the driver's side door of the truck, advertising a landscaping company. A man exited the pickup, waved at Silas and Zayn before heading up to the front door of the house and opening the door for the movers. The man then walked over to introduce himself to his new neighbors.

"Hello gentlemen. I'm Jaxon Pierce," the man said, shaking their hands.

Jaxon Pierce was built like the 1970s adult movie actor, Ron Jeremy. He stood at an average five feet, six inches and appeared to be 150 pounds overweight. He was wearing a pair of denim shorts and a short sleeved, buttoned down dress shirt, which was only buttoned up to his sternum, revealing the wool sweater like covering of chest hair.

"I'm Silas Graham and this is Zayn Miller. I live across the street," Silas told him.

"How about you have a seat here and tell us about

yourself," Zayn suggested.

Zayn stood up and offered his chair to the new neighbor. As Jaxon accepted the seat, Zayn walked over to his garage to retrieve another chair and returned to join the other men.

"My parents have always wanted to make sure I have kept busy. As a child, I played several different sports to ensure that I kept busy. When I decided to start my own landscaping business my junior year of high school, my parents were upset that I didn't want to go to college. I felt that if I started my own company young, I would have enough money to be on my own early in adulthood," Jaxon began, after Silas passed him an open beer.

"That sounds like a very lucrative business plan for a young man," Zayn told him, tipping his beer toward Jaxon.

"By my senior year, I had figured out how to make my own fertilizer. I originally started with rats and small rodents, removing their insides and pouring different chemicals inside their hollowed out bodies to ensure quick decomposition. I would wrap up the organs, then cook them to feed to my dog. I had figured out the mixture of drain clog remover and heavy duty carbon remover would practically liquify the remains.

"I had started with a compost pile that I was throwing the carcasses of the animals into. Mixing the remains with fruit and vegetable garbage in the compost pile actually masked the smell of the rotting flesh a little. By the time I was twenty-five, I had begun producing my own landscaping fertilizer, which I would use in my business.

"My parents had decided that my fertilizer pile was becoming an eyesore on their property, so I decided it was time to get my own home. That's when I found the perfect home in a quiet cul-de-sac with a large field behind it where I could produce my fertilizer and continue my business," Jaxon concluded.

"You seem to be doing well for yourself," Silas commented.

What Jaxon didn't divulge to his new neighbors was that he had moved from small rodents to humans. He would find homeless people or ladies of the night because he figured no one would be looking for them and those kind of people disappeared all the time.

"I hope the smell doesn't bother either of you. The pile I have that still sits on my parents property is being delivered later this week. Also, if you have any food trash, please let me know. I would love to add it to my compost pile," Jaxon told his neighbors.

"I could keep a secondary container for those things and bring it over to you when it's full. How about you Zayn?" Silas offered.

"That sounds great. I would love to help. I know a compost pile can actually help the environment. Less trash in the land fills and things that come from the earth go back into the earth," Zayn said.

"Thank you. I'm so glad I chose this home. I promise to be a great neighbor. Just let me know if the smell gets to you and I will try to figure out something to make it more pleasant. Let me finish with the movers and I'll come back out," Jaxon told them.

Silas and Zayn were happy to have a great neighbor move onto the street. Before Michelle's house sold, Karen would stop by daily to visit with her friends. If Zayn was outside, the three ladies would stroll over to tell him that Silas was a sexual deviant.

As Michelle packed her children into her minivan on the day her family moved out, all three women were standing on her driveway as Zayn exited his home. They shouted vile things about Silas, as well as homophobic slurs at him.

Initially, he just ignored them; that was until Karen shouted that God hates gays. That was when he told the women to mind their own business and to just hurry and move the fuck out. After that, Karen stopped coming by and Cybil decided she would stay with Karen until her house sold.

Cybil told her husband that she no longer felt safe in the home with their children. He decided to remain in the home alone, as he felt the women were overreacting. Technically, Cybil's husband had decided to separate from her and he was not in any hurry to sell the house.

When the moving truck was pulling away from Jaxon's house, Cybil's husband was driving down the street heading home from work. Within a few moments, Karen's husband, the real estate agent, pulled into the driveway of the home next to Silas.

Karen's husband exited the driver's side of the vehicle and a young man exited the passenger side. Silas, Zayn and Jaxon were sitting on the driveway of Zayn's house, watching the three men as they entered the home.

"What do we think of this guy?" Silas asked.

"He's a little young, but he couldn't be any worse than the horrible women who used to live here," Zayn said.

"Could they really have been that bad?" Jaxon asked.

Before they could answer, Cybil's husband stepped out of the home and headed over to Zayn's home. Silas, Jaxon and Zayn all stood as he approached.

"Hey guys. I'm George, Cybil's husband. Silas, I'm sorry the ladies were very unwelcoming towards you. Their anger was unnecessarily aimed at you. Cybil was generally angry at me, due to the fact that I would consistently work late. Karen was angry at her husband because he paid more attention to his phone and clients, than he did to her. I wish we could have been able to get to know each other before it had escalated to this point."

"I really appreciate your kindness. It's strange how someone so accepting of alternative lifestyles could have married such a close-minded person," Silas told George.

"She wasn't always a bitch, it's just gotten worse as the kids get older. She doesn't want our son to be gay and she's afraid that if he sees someone who is, eventually he will mimic the mannerisms until he turns gay. No matter how many times I tell her that's not how it works, she still insists that young boys can catch the gay," George said, rolling his eyes at the ridiculousness of the narrative.

"Well then, I guess it's a good thing that she took the kids and left when she did. I was planning on recruiting new gays next week and I think your son would make a good gay," Silas joked.

The four men laughed and Silas was glad that George understood he was joking. When Karen's husband and the young man exited Cybil and George's home, George shook hands with Silas, Zayn and Jaxon before returning to his home in order to speak with the realtor and the potential buyer.

"So how bad were these ladies, really? You have to tell me now. That guy just called his wife a bitch," Jaxon practically begged, after they had returned to their seats.

Silas and Zayn went through all the instances of when they had come into contact with the horrible women. Jaxon was stunned that some people were unwilling to evolve with the times and were stuck in the past.

"What happened to love thy neighbor? Or the great saying that if you don't have anything nice to say, don't say anything at all? There are so many people in this world who need to accept the differences of all people and not shun those that are different," Jaxon stated.

"You should be a politician. Maybe you could bring this country together, rather than causing the segregation that is happening right now," Zayn said.

"I think the biggest problem is some people seem

to think they are victims, when in actuality they are the ones who are victimizing themselves. If they would just live their lives and be nice to others around them, there would be more people willing to accept strangers for who they are, rather than vilifying people who are actually good at heart," Silas preached.

"Wow, that was insightful," Jaxon said, nodding his head.

"Being a gay man, I have been labeled a villain most of my life," Silas explained.

"That makes sense. There are too many people that are unwilling to accept differences in the world. If everyone was the same, the world would be a boring place," Jaxon said.

Eight

Within the next couple of days, the realtor sign was removed from Cybil's house. Silas, Zayn and Jaxon waited to see who their new neighbor was going to be. Since George was still living in the home, it was the full thirty days before he had completely moved out. George left on a Wednesday and that following Friday, a caravan of pickup trucks pulled up to the house next door to Silas.

Jaxon and Zayn jogged over to Silas' house to inform him of the new neighbor. The three men decided to sit on the driveway of Silas' house and watch.

"So which one of these young guys do you think is the homeowner?" Jaxon asked.

"Maybe they all own the house," Zayn said.

"Let's just hope it's not going to be a party house," Silas said.

"That would not be good. I don't want a bunch of drunk people playing in my fertilizer piles," Jaxon said, gnawing on the side of his thumbnail.

"I wouldn't want them messing up my flowerbeds in the back," Silas said.

"I guess we will see. None of them so far has even acknowledged the fact that we are sitting here, so maybe they will just keep to themselves," Zayn said.

"I could always call my friends over and have Frankie cat call the guys, just to make sure they aren't homophobic," Silas suggested.

"As much fun as that would be, I would rather just

sit here and hope that maybe the new neighbor keeps to themselves," Jaxon said.

"I agree. I don't care who owns the house, but whoever it is, I hope they mind their own business," Zayn said.

For the following three months, every Friday and Saturday night, their new neighbor had fraternity style parties. Several drunk people would be found in the morning on the front lawn of the party house and cars would be parked all over the cul-de-sac. Silas, Zayn and Jaxon would rotate as to which house they would meet at those nights because they knew if they had left the neighborhood, they would be blocked from returning to their homes.

There were several times Silas had to poke at the hungover party guests that had decided to pass out on his front lawn. They would groan, roll on to their side and vomit the poison they had ingested from the party. As a courtesy, he would assist them back to the house next door, leaving them on the doorstep. Jaxon and Silas suffered more than Zayn with the unwanted visitors, as they lived on either side of the party house and their front lawns all basically moulded together.

Their new neighbor never bothered to introduce himself in the three months that he had thrown his elaborate parties, but Silas, Zayn and Jaxon never made a point to introduce themselves to him either. They were sure only one person was living in the house and they were sure the owner was male, but they were wondering what exactly was going on behind closed doors.

During the week the house was quiet with only single female visitors coming and going. Several daily, but never overlapping the visits. At one time, the men thought their new neighbor was either being paid by these women, or was paying the women, but as time went on they assumed he was just convincing young naïve girls to give their innocence to him.

"Have either of you noticed how many women this guy brings home?" Zayn asked.

"I know how many show up for his parties," Jaxon said.

"I know how many guys have come over. A couple of them have noticed me," Silas said, raising his eyebrows.

"Have you encouraged any of them to come over?" Zayn wanted to know.

"Well, I have tried, but so far none of them have made their way over," Silas informed.

"I can tell you, those party visitors are encroaching over the property line and are becoming a nuisance," Jaxon said.

"I think that the only problem I have is that I would like to leave my home on Friday because I have a date. I would also like to bring my date home for a little extracurricular activities," Silas told them. "I don't know how much longer I can go without my extracurricular activities."

"I know that feeling, but with my mother in the house, I can't bring home my girlfriend. She understands and has her own home that we meet at twice a week, but I don't ever stay the night just in case my mother needs me," Zayn said.

"If you ever want to stay over at your girlfriend's house, just let me know. Your mother and Frankie get along really well. I know he would love to spend extra time with her. His parents disowned him when he came out and she told him if he ever needed motherly guidance that she would be there for him," Silas said.

"Is that why he calls her almost every night?" Zayn inquired.

"Probably. I know he calls her Momma Edna," Silas told him.

"That's sweet. Your friends are great guys," Jaxon added his input.

"Maybe we should talk to him this weekend and see if he could possibly tone down the parties to once a month," Zayn suggested.

"Do you think that talking to him would help?" Silas asked.

Silas was hitting his breaking point. He needed to kill someone and reach his release. Not knowing when the opportunity would present itself in order for him to strangle his next victim, Silas was becoming agitated.

Zayn was going to have time off from his job and had already chosen his next victim. He didn't really have a girlfriend, but he had been meeting with a woman whose husband was becoming increasingly more and more violent and she was providing Zayn with photos and proof that was just fueling the fire within him.

Jaxon had to pass up his usual weekly drifter, due to the disruption from his neighbor. He created a chart and tried to plan it out, but as each Friday would come and the party goers would begin to show up, Jaxon's plan was thrown out. There was no way that he could bring a potential victim into his home without someone noticing. His compost pile was suffering and all he wanted was fertilization of a decomposing body mixed within.

As the end of the week once again approached, Silas, Zayn and Jaxon came up with a plan on how to confront their new neighbor. They were going to try to talk to him as he pulled up when he got home from what they assumed was his job. They figured if they talked to him before the party, then maybe there was still time to have it canceled.

When that Friday came around, their new neighbor never left his house and no one had come over.

The sounds however, coming from his garage, sounded as though he was remodeling.

"What do you think he is doing in there?" Zayn asked Jaxon, as they walked over to Silas' house.

"Maybe he's turning it into another room?" Jaxon suggested.

"Hopefully this means he isn't having a party tonight," Zayn said, as he knocked on the front door to Silas' house.

"What is going on next door?" Silas asked, as he opened his door and saw his neighbors standing on his doorstep.

"Possibly some kind of renovation?" Jaxon shrugged.

"Hopefully this means I can bring my date home and he's not going to have his party tonight, but we should still go talk to him," Silas said.

"The plan was to talk to him later tonight. Do I need to rewrite the plan, so we can go talk to him now?" Jaxon asked, sounding panicked.

"Relax Jaxon. Plans can always be changed," Zayn told him, patting Jaxon on the shoulder.

"Not without possible consequences. If plans change, then the whole day is thrown off," Jaxon ranted.

"Well, let's go talk to him now and the rest of your day can continue as planned, but without the conversation," Zayn told Jaxon.

The three men walked over to the new neighbor's house. Zayn was the first to step up to the door. He turned to look at the others before he raised his hand and knocked.

Nine

After a few moments, when the sounds of the power tools didn't stop, Silas then reached over and rang the doorbell. They didn't hear the sound of the bell, but the power tools stopped.

It only took seconds before the front door swung open and a young gentleman stood in the foyer. He was dressed in a muscle shirt and denim shorts, with a tool belt around his waist. Sweat glistened across his forehead and down his scrawny arms. He appeared strong, but in the sense that he probably lifted heavy objects during a party while his drunk friends encouraged juvenile behavior.

"What do you want?" the young man said, placing a fist on his hip.

"Hello, sir. We are your neighbors and we just wanted to introduce ourselves," Jaxon said, extending his hand.

"Oh, well okay. I'm Evander Thompson. You guys want to come in?" the new neighbor said, shaking Jaxon's hand.

"Thank you. I'm Jaxon Pierce, this is Zayn Miller and Silas Graham."

"I was wondering if you guys were going to come over. I see y'all talking all the time, but you have never come over to talk to me. I thought y'all were a part of a group that you didn't want me to be a part of," Evander said, as he led the other men to his dining room table.

"Well, since you have moved in, you have had some serious parties on a regular basis and we aren't exactly the party type of guys," Zayn told him.

"I don't throw parties all day every day. You could have come over at any time," Evander said, defensively.

"Look, we have to live here together. We need to be civil towards each other. Is there any way that you could slow down on the partying? With all the vehicles that gather up and down the street, we are basically trapped in our homes," Silas said, calmly.

"Don't worry. My friends just wanted to make sure I had the best house warming party and it lasted a little longer than anticipated," Evander informed.

"So the parties are over?" Jaxon asked.

"Yes, the parties are over. I have a private life that my friends wouldn't understand," Evander said, looking down at his feet and running his fingers through his hair.

"I think we all have private lives that our day to day friends wouldn't understand. How about you tell us a little bit about you," Zayn encouraged Evander to open up, as they all sat down around the table.

Evander retrieved four bottles of water from his refrigerator and placed them in the center of the table before he began. "Well, I'm the oldest of two boys. My parents basically treated me like I was the practice child and my younger brother could do no wrong.

"For several years I thought I was adopted, since my parents basically treated me like an outsider. I have never felt accepted, not just by my parents, but also by other members of my family. By the time I was fourteen, I had developed a short temper. I have never had a problem making friends, but as for romantic relationships, I haven't been able to find anyone who has wanted to be more than friends."

"But we see women coming and going from your house all the time," Silas said, confused.

"Did you ever find out if you were adopted?" Jaxon inquired.

"I only thought I was adopted from the time my brother was born when I was eight years old, until the time I had turned thirteen. By the time he was five, I noticed how much we looked alike and knew that it was a long shot if I had been adopted. As for the ladies you see coming and going, I have someone who stops by daily and cleans my house.

"Every Monday and Thursday I have a private masseur come by. Sometimes she gives me a little extra rubbing and sometimes I call friend over to assist with that," Evander said, raising his eyebrows and smirking.

"There have been a few times I have seen up to five women enter and exit your home in one day," Zayn inquired.

"Okay look, sometimes I like a little foreplay before slamming it in. I call over a few girls who allow me to do things to them. They are dominant and tell me what to do to them, but they never do anything to me. The last girl is more submissive and she's the one I finish with," Evander explained, crossing his arms over his chest and tucking his hands into his armpits as he peered down at his feet.

"Gross. I could have gone my entire life without hearing about that," Silas said, curling up the right side of his upper lip.

"That was more information than was necessary. So what do you do for work, Evander?" Jaxon asked, changing the subject.

"I work part time at a retail store. I stock the shelves and shit, but basically do as little as possible, so they won't ask me to do too much," Evander said.

"How are you able to afford the mortgage on this home with part time pay?" Zayn wondered.

"My parents are rich. I turned twenty one a few months ago and they told me they wanted me to move out. I got a job, but it didn't pay enough for me to move out. My dad told me that as long as I kept my job, he would pay all my household bills and all I have to pay for is my own food. The masseur has been on a standing appointment since I turned eighteen. It is the only nice thing my parents have ever given me," Evander stated.

"That's the most entitled, spoiled brat thing I have ever heard anyone say. I'm out of here," Silas said, as he stood and headed for the front door.

"I have to agree with Silas. I feel like your friends are only your friends because your parents are rich,"

Zayn said, as the other two stood and followed Silas out of the house.

"Yeah, your personality is absolutely entitled. We are willing to be cordial towards you, but we won't ever invite you over to hang out with us," Jaxon said, from Evander's front porch.

"That's fine. Fuck you guys," Evander said, before slamming his front door closed and locking it.

Evander was fuming. He had opened up and told his neighbors about his personal life. Of course, he wasn't planning to share about his secret life. He knew that he came on a little strong with girls; always had. When his friends began dating girls in their early teen years, he was unable to find any girl willing to be his girlfriend.

As his temper began to flair, any time a girl seemed to pay attention to him, Evander would become obsessive and clingy. His behavior would scare off the possibility of a relationship after only a couple of days. When he was seventeen, he claimed his first victim.

Evander was on a two week vacation with his

family. After arriving at the hotel the first day, he told his parents he was going to go lounge by the indoor pool. While there, he noticed a young girl sitting at the edge of the pool, dangling her feet in the water.

He walked over and sat down approximately three feet away from her and dangled his feet in the water as well. She looked over at him and smiled.

"I'm Evander," he told her, smiling back.

"I'm Hailey," the girl said, inching closer to him.

"I'm sixteen," he lied, knowing that the girl was much younger.

He became aroused when she told him she was only thirteen. Due to her young age and naïvety, he was sure he would be able to manipulate her. She had engaged him in conversation and he felt that she was flirting with him.

They only talked for about half an hour before she stood up and said she had to go meet her parents for dinner, as she shuffled away from the pool area. After their initial meeting, he made sure to run into Hailey everyday. After a couple of days, he was obsessed with her and made sure he knew when she was going to be in the hotel. Once she had revealed what she would be doing with her parents, anytime he saw her at the hotel, he would follow her around. If she was alone, he would approach her, but if she was with her parents he would just creep around, watching her from a distance.

At the end of the first week, Evander spotted Hailey alone, late one night in the hallway. He approached her, placing his hands on her hips, as if they were in a relationship.

"Where are you going?" he asked, as she backed away from his touch.

"I was going down to the pool area," she told him.

"Would you like some company?" he asked.

"I guess," she said, reluctantly.

The two of them strolled through the halls of the hotel, before riding the elevator down to the pool area. Evander was glad to see they were alone, as they sat on the edge of the pool, with their legs dangling down in the water.

"We should go swimming in our underwear," he suggested.

"No, I don't want to do that," Hailey said, as she became uncomfortable and stood up.

As she quickly walked toward the exit of the pool area, Evander jumped up onto his feet and stopped her from leaving. He grabbed her by the arm and spun her around to face him, pulling her away from the door. She yelled at him that she wanted him to leave her alone and tried pulling her arm from his grasp. He was making her feel uneasy and she felt as though he was being creepy.

"You're going to regret that," he told Hailey, as he became enraged with her.

With a quick motion, Evander wrapped his hands around her neck squeezing her trachea until she passed out. As her body went limp, he hooked his elbows under her armpits and dragged her unconscious body into the pool maintenance room. He laid her body down on the floor and found a flat head screwdriver sitting on top of a tool cabinet.

He grasped the screwdriver in his hand and plunged it into her torso over and over again. Every time he swung the weapon back over his head, before jamming it back into her body, blood would fling around onto every surface in the room.

To be sure he had snuffed out her life, he placed the tip of the tool into the soft flesh directly above where her collar bones met just under the esophagus and slammed the heel of his hand down on the screwdriver's handle, feeling the weapon slide all the way through and exit out the back of her neck..

Leaving the tool protruding from her neck, Evander stood over the young girl's body and admired what he had just done. One corner of his mouth curled up from crude enjoyment and he became overly aroused by the blood splattered all over the small room.

He glared down at the body as he pleasured himself by rubbing his erection over his pants. Once he had climaxed and the ooze of the substance that had released from his shaft was pooling in his underwear, he decided the scene no longer excited him. He was now bored and wanted to go back to the hotel room.

Evander left her body in the maintenance room, snuck out and closed the door. Due to the fact that he was covered in the young girl's blood, he jumped into the pool in order to rinse off his hands, arms and what he could off his clothes.

His clothing was dripping as he headed back to the room he shared with his younger brother. His parents had booked adjoining rooms for them and he was glad he didn't see anyone else wandering the hallways.

His brother was already asleep when he arrived. Evander removed his wet clothing, stuffed them in a plastic bag with a drawstring top that was provided in the hotel room and stuffed the bag into his luggage.

As he showered, he practically danced around in the water. After lathering up with the supplied bar of soap, he rinsed and turned off the water. Evander wasn't sure how long he had been in the shower, but as he wrapped a towel around his waist, there was a knock on the room door. He grabbed another towel and rubbed it in his hair, just to be sure he had got all the blood out.

Noticing the towel remained white, he dropped it on the floor in the bathroom, before he opened the door in order to find out who was knocking. Hailey's parents stood on the other side. He had seen them when he was stalking her, but Evander was sure they had never seen him.

"Have you seen this girl?" her dad asked, holding up a picture of Hailey, as her mother cried.

"No, I haven't seen her. We are on vacation with our parents," Evander denied, using his fake, respectful tone.

"We have been in this room since we got back from dinner," his brother said from behind him.

Evander was thankful his brother had provided him with an alibi. Hailey's parents accepted their answers and moved to the room across the hall. He closed the door and locked it, as his brother went back to bed. Evander dressed before getting comfortable in the other bed, turned on the television and waited for the discovery of the girl's body.

By mid-morning, the next day, everyone in the hotel knew about the young girl found dead in the pool maintenance room. He was questioned by the police, but everyone at the hotel was questioned. After her parents had gone room to room the night before, asking everyone if they had seen her, they had gone to the front desk and the hotel manager had contacted the police.

The fact that no one in the hotel had seen the two of them together, Evander was not a suspect. He felt powerful because he was able to stalk this girl and murder her without anyone knowing what he had done.

After his first victim, Evander knew he had to make sure he wasn't memorable enough for anyone who would have seen him together with his victims. He wanted to be sure no one would be able to pick him out of a lineup.

No one saw him take his first victim into the maintenance room and no one saw him jump into the pool. Since he had managed to commit murder and get away with it the first time, nothing could stop him from killing again.

That was when he would become sexually aroused while he was out hunting for his victims, as well as after when he was admiring his work. Being a retail associate, he had a flexible schedule in order to continue with his sadistic hobby.

He preferred leaving his victims out in the open to be discovered. It was his way of showing off his work to everyone who saw the body and it excited him every time he got away with it.

By the time Evander had graduated from high school, he was using the shed in the backyard at his parents house to cut open his victims, remove their insides and fill their bodies with random objects. In the middle of the night he would pack the body into his vehicle, leave the house and dump the body in a secluded area.

He was glad when his neighbors left his house. He didn't really want to tell them anything else about his personal life and wasn't too keen to know anything about them either. He just wanted to go back out to his garage and finish building his dissection room.

Jaxon, Zayn and Silas had headed down Evander's driveway and walked toward Silas' house. The three men were still fuming from their interaction with their neighbor.

"Well, that was rude," Silas said, as he opened his

front door.

"He seems a little young. Hopefully he will come around and be more neighborly," Jaxon stated.

"I don't give a shit what he does, as long as he minds his own damn business," Silas said, gruffly as they entered his home.

"We have to live next to him, so hopefully at some point he becomes more friendly," Zayn said.

Jaxon and Zayn sat down on the sofa as Silas retreated to the kitchen to grab a six pack of beer. The men sat around complaining about their new neighbor well into the night. Once they all were three sheets to the wind, Jaxon and Zayn stumbled off to their homes, as Silas decided to hunker down on his sofa.

Ten

The next morning, Silas had breakfast and coffee before he planned out the location of his next target. He was thankful that Evander's parties were over. He pulled out the state map he kept in his kitchen's junk drawer and spread it out on his dining room table. There was a small town almost four hours away, but the population was small enough that he was afraid if someone disappeared, they would be missed.

He decided to move about thirty minutes north of that town, to a small city. The population was significantly more dense and most likely, one person missing wouldn't be noticed.

Silas packed his stakeout bag with snacks and water, before heading out for the long drive. After placing the bag on the front passenger seat, he decides he is going to also pack an overnight bag for a couple of days. He figured it could take a couple days to find the right target within the over 250,000 people.

He tossed his overnight bag in the trunk of his car, then drove out of the neighborhood. He went over his perfect victim checklist in his head as he made the long drive. The number one was, of course, they have to be a gay man. That was a guarantee that Silas would get lucky.

As Silas entered the city limits, he began searching for a place to stake out in order to choose a target. He passed over several bars due to the fact that they were packed with people and he didn't want to give the opportunity to possibly being seen leaving with someone.

Eventually, he found a bar tucked away from the road. There was a small sign in the shape of an arrow, attached to a wooden stake with the word 'BAR' written in red across the arrow. The sign was pointing down a dirt road.

Silas turned off the pavement and followed the winding trail approximately three quarters of a mile to where it dead ended. At the end was a grassy area where ten vehicles were parked. There was also a very run down looking building with a light up sign which read 'BAR' that stood on top of the front patio covered roof.

He found a spot away from the front doors to park. As he pressed the ignition button, turning off the engine, Silas took a survey of his surroundings. He wanted to make sure no one would spot him exiting the vehicle. Once he was positive there were no other patrons around, he exited his vehicle and headed up to the entrance.

It was a small building with booths lined up along

the wall to the right of the entrance, as well as to the left with a corner booth to the left and three more around the side wall past the corner booth. A few round tables occupied the center of the room with four chairs at each table. The wall opposite from the entrance had a door indicating where the restrooms were located and a rectangular passthrough window which looked into the kitchen area. In front of the kitchen area was the wet bar where the drinks were made.

There were seven patrons occupying the seating area. Four men sat at one round table, two women occupied one booth and one man sat alone at a booth. Silas chose a booth on the opposite side from the lone gentleman. He ordered a beer from the server who approached him as soon as he sat down.

Once the beer was delivered, Silas observed the man without rousing suspicion. The server had called the man by name a couple of times, so Silas was aware that his name was Stuart.

After Stuart had consumed three beers, he dropped a few dollar bills onto the table and verbalized a farewell to the employees of the establishment as he stood and headed out of the bar. Silas took one last sip of his beer before placing payment on the table and exiting as well.

Stuart was just opening the door to an old beat up pickup truck, when Silas spotted him. Silas quickly made his way to his vehicle and prepared to follow Stuart to his next location. After pulling out of the parking area and a fifteen minute drive, Stuart pulled up to a house with only the outside patio lights illuminated.

Silas was positive Stuart lived alone as he watched lights turn on and off, presumably that his target was headed to bed. After the house was dark, Silas decided to find a hotel for a few hours, then return just before the break of dawn.

Over the next few weeks, Silas spent most nights getting to know his next victim. He hadn't approached Stuart yet, but he knew where he worked, lived and the places he frequented.

Stuart seemed to be a loner. He worked in a call center where he sat in a cubical and answered the phone all day. He even ate lunch alone in his pickup truck and after work, he would stop at the same bar, on his way home. He would sip a couple of beers from the same booth, before slipping out and going home, alone.

Every third day, Silas would drive out to watch as Stuart would drink his two beers. He tried to get Stuart to notice him from across the bar, but Stuart never looked up from the newspaper he would read daily.

On the weekends, other patrons would pack into the pub. As each table became occupied, the bartender would set up six barstools lined along the bar he stood behind making drinks and Stuart would leave and head home. Silas would then watch Stuart from his car parked at the curb out in front of the house. The curtains in the front window were parted just enough that Silas could see Stuart have a few more beers, while sitting on his sofa watching television.

After the two beers at the bar, then three more at home, Stuart would order dinner from a delivery service. Once he would finish eating, Stuart would put away any leftovers before turning off the tv and heading into his bedroom. Silas couldn't see the bedroom from his car, so he would imagine Stuart getting naked and taking a shower before going to bed. Once the house was dark and there wasn't any noticeable movement inside, Silas would head home.

For four months Silas had continued his stalking cycle hoping that Stuart would eventually join him in the booth at the bar, but it seemed that Silas would have to make the first move. He spent the following several weeks trying to devise a plan to approach his victim. Due to the fact that Stuart was a loner, Silas was worried that it could be difficult to approach him, but it could also be perfect for Silas. That way, Stuart wouldn't be missed once he was gone and it would possibly take longer before anyone noticed he was missing. Unfortunately, that also meant that he would most likely be harder to encourage to go home with Silas.

Silas was becoming more and more sexually frustrated as time went on. Knowing who his target was and basically being prepared for the final act, his frustrations were building. He wanted to take this man home and tie him up. He also felt a slight connection with Stuart, even though he hadn't talked to him.

Every time he had chosen a target, after his first, they had always approached him. It had been several years since he had initiated a conversation with a target and he was nervous to even attempt.

Silas even thought about keeping Stuart around for a couple of days, just playing out a few fantasy rolls, before strangling him, but he knew that could be risky. He just wanted to play with Stuart as though he were a life-sized doll and wondered if maybe Stuart would be willing to play with him.

As Silas drove home one night after eating alone at a local restaurant, he decided to call Derik to see if he would come over for a little relief. He needed to let loose and he knew Derik would humor him with sexy roll play.

"Hey Derik, it's Silas," he said, into his cell phone.

"Hello Silas. It's a little late. Are you okay?" Derik inquired.

"I was just wondering if you would like to come over. I'm feeling a little randy and would appreciate some assistance," Silas informed.

"I understand. Anything specific you want me to wear?"

"Surprise me, but make sure it's something that will drive me crazy."

"I know just the thing. I'll be there in twenty minutes."

Silas hung up and rubbed his crotch as he pulled into his driveway. He felt sparks with Derik and really wanted to have a relationship with him in the future, but he wasn't sure if Derik could handle his extracurricular activities. It was the one aspect of his life he never wanted to reveal to his friends and he didn't want to continue once he was prepared to settle down.

As he exited his vehicle and headed up to his front door, he heard someone approaching behind him. Silas turned around to see Zayn headed his way.

"Hey neighbor. You wouldn't mind if my mother spent the night with you, would you?" Zayn asked.

"Tonight?" Silas questioned, worried his plans for the evening were about to be ruined.

"It's late tonight. I meant tomorrow night. I wanted to bring my girlfriend over and didn't think it would be respectful, if we get intimate, to have my mother in the house."

"Oh, yeah that's fine. I do have Derik coming over now and would like to prepare for that, so I'll see you tomorrow."

"I gotcha. No problem. Thank you."

Zayn backed away and jogged across the street, back to his house. Silas waited until his neighbor had disappeared behind his front door, before he entered his home.

Silas set up a few candles in his living room and placed one in the center of the dining room table. Dimming the lights, he then headed to his room to change into something easily removable.

As soon as Silas was retrieving a bottle of wine and two wine glasses from the kitchen, there was a knock on his front door. He walked toward the living room, wine and glasses in hand and set them down on the coffee table, before walking over to open the door. Derik was standing on the door step, wearing a trench coat.

"Did someone order a stripper?" Derik said, as he raised his eyebrows and slyly smiled, stepping into the house.

"I sure did," Silas responded, licking his lips, standing in front of Derik wearing only athletic shorts. "Would you like to take off your coat?"

"You pour the wine and I will get more comfortable," Derik said, closing and locking the door.

Silas picked up the wine glasses, one by one and filled each about half way, as Derik removed the trench coat and draped it over the back of the sofa. Derik was standing in front of Silas wearing a black silk thong and nothing else. Silas bit his bottom lip and handed Derik one of the glasses of wine.

The two men sat down on the sofa, sipped their wine and glared at each other seductively. It didn't take long before Derik placed his glass down on the coffee table. He stood up and took the glass from Silas as well, setting it next to the other. Derik leaned down to kiss Silas slowly, then turned around and proceeded to perform a lap dance for Silas.

Eleven

The next morning, when Silas woke up, he was laying in his bed. His head was on Derik's shoulder, his hand on Derik's chest and their legs were intertwined. Silas gently kissed Derik's bicep, as he slid his hand down to Derik's groin.

"Oh, are you looking for an encore?" Derik asked,

as he shifted his pelvis.

"How about a thank you for last night," Silas said, pressing his lips against Derik's nipple.

"Is this going to be a regular occurrence, or just a one off?" Derik asked.

"I don't know. Can we just enjoy each other in this moment?"

"Silas, I really like you and would like to have a relationship with you, not just relations."

"My life is really complicated right now. I don't feel like I can give you the attention a relationship needs."

"I get it. Can I borrow some clothes, so I don't have to leave here in a trench coat," Derik said, frustrated, sitting up on the side of the bed.

Silas leaned across the bed and ran his finger up and down along Derik's spine. "I really like you, Derik. You just deserve better than me. I'm not the kind of guy who can give you the attention you deserve."

"Just give me something to wear, so I can leave," Derik insisted, standing.

Silas rolled up into a sitting position and rubbed

his face. "Please don't be upset. I'll make you breakfast and we can talk. Maybe we can turn this into a regular meeting," Silas told him, before standing and pulling out an undershirt and athletic shorts from his dresser.

"You have got to be kidding me. Are you trying to turn this into a business transaction?" Derik wanted to know, as he pulled on the clothing.

"No, that's not what I meant. Please stay for breakfast."

"I really like you, Silas. I have liked you for years. Hell, I'm sure that I'm in *love* with you. In case you haven't noticed, I have been waiting for you to come around and haven't dated anyone since I started having feelings for you."

Derik headed out toward the living room to retrieve his coat and thong on his way out. Silas sat down on his bed and began re-evaluating his life choices, as he heard Derik slam the front door. He believed eventually he could be the partner Derik deserved, but once his sights were set on a victim, he had to follow through.

Silas stood up and headed to his shower. He cleaned up and dressed for the day, preparing for his next overnight guest.

Later that afternoon, Zayn stopped by with Edna and they had brought lunch. Silas was glad to have the distraction because he had felt bad about the interaction he had with Derik.

"Thank you so much for allowing me to stay with you tonight. I feel bad that Zayn doesn't get to have a social life because he is taking care of me," Edna told Silas.

"No problem Mrs. Edna. We can play games tonight and allow Zayn to have a nice evening with his lady friend," Silas said.

"Nice evening huh. I know what he is going to be doing over there, but at least he gets to do it longer than a quickie in the middle of the afternoon," Edna said, giggling.

"Mom, don't say things like that," Zayn sighed and rolled his eyes.

"You act like I don't know. Some days you come home in a better mood than others. I know what you are doing," Edna told him, wagging her finger.

"That's not what I'm always doing when I come home in a good mood. I have other activities that I enjoy," Zayn argued.

"Oh yeah? Like what?" Edna wanted to know.

"I kill people. It's a great stress reliever," Zayn told her, nonchalantly.

"Yeah right. And I do gymnastics right after my chemo treatments. It helps with the nausea," Edna said, scoffing.

Silas laughed at the interaction, but wondered how serious Zayn was with his statement. He wanted to ask about it, but wouldn't in front of Edna. It would have to be an anomaly in order for there to be more than one killer to be living in the same neighborhood, let alone on the same street.

After lunch, Edna decided she was going to take a nap, so Silas pushed her in her wheelchair to his guest room. He had made the bed with nice sheets and meticulously cleaned everything, as well as put in an air freshener to create a nice scent before they had arrived. Stopping the wheelchair beside the bed, he assisted her transition from the chair to the bed. He made sure to close the bedroom door on his way out, so she wouldn't hear the serious conversation Silas wanted to have with Zayn.

"Zayn, I have to ask you an important question and I want the truth," Silas said, once he had returned to the dining room.

"Sure buddy. What's up?" Zayn said.

"Did you mean it when you said you kill people? I want the truth. I'm not going to turn you in, or anything. I just want to know," Silas inquired.

"It was just a joke. My mother has that kind of sense of humor. I knew she would think it was funny," Zayn lied.

"It didn't sound like a joke. It sounded like a sort of confession. Almost as if you want to tell someone, but you don't know who you can trust. You can trust me," Silas told him, raising his eyebrows.

"I don't know what you are talking about. My mother and I both have a dark sense of humor and sometimes I make a joke with her that I kill people. She never takes me seriously and we always laugh about it."

"Sometimes the things we say when we are joking are actually the truth."

Zayn stared at Silas for a moment. He looked deep into Silas' eyes and felt as though Silas was communicating with him telepathically. He felt connected, as if he really could trust Silas with his deep dark secret.

"Will this stay just between us?" Zayn asked.

"Just us. I promise."

"Remember when I told you about how my dad used to beat on my mom? While she was in the hospital recovering, I killed him. She doesn't know that's the reason he disappeared. Watching my mother get beaten, on a regular basis by a man who felt as though he had the right because they were married and she belonged to him, had really unleashed a burning rage inside me.

"After that, I vowed to protect all women against abusive husbands. Sometimes I am contacted by the victim, other times I am contacted by a friend or family member of the victim. I also have a contact at the local hospital that lets me know when a woman comes in with injuries inflicted by her husband."

"What if the woman is lying?"

"I investigate the suspect first. If I find anything that suggests he is involved in domestic violence, I take him out."

"Are you a cop?" Silas wanted to know.

"Not a cop, but I do private investigations on the side. I don't ask for payment, but if the victim thinks I am a private investigator who is going to scare their husband out of their life, they are more willing to talk to me. If I come right out and say I am a hired hit man, it's less likely they will go along with it," Zayn informed.

"That's nice. It's good to know there is someone out there to protect the victim."

"Your turn."

"What do you mean?"

"Now it's your turn to tell me something that you have never told anyone else in your life. That way I know you won't tell. You have something on me, now I need something on you."

"Okay, so what are the odds that there are two

killers living on the same street?" Silas asked.

"Wait, you too?" Zayn inquired.

"The only difference between your targets and mine, is that your targets deserve what they get. I stalk lonely gay men, bring them back to my house and strangle them during a sexual encounter."

"What about the man that the women who used to live in these homes saw you bring home?"

"Buried under the flowers in the backyard," Silas told him, pointing out the back window that looked out to the garden.

"Well damn. You like to keep them close. I dump my guys all over. Aren't you afraid of getting caught doing that?" Zayn asked.

"Naw, the body is buried deep enough to keep the smell of decay to a minimum, if at all and the flowers explain the fresh dirt."

"How often do you do this?"

"Only twice a year. That way I don't draw too much attention to myself. How about you?"

"Quarterly. I have a building that is registered to my investigation business as an office. It's actually set up just like an office. I even have employees that help with background checks. There is one room in that building that doesn't have any windows. That's the room where I meet with them, snuff them out, dismember the bodies, then distribute the parts in several different disposal bags."

"You go through a lot of steps just to get rid of the trash," Silas said.

"Yeah, but there isn't any connection to me in any way when the skeletal remains surface," Zayn said.

"I guess that's a bonus. Although, if the bodies in my yard surface, there isn't really any connection between them and me. For all I know, those bodies were buried there when I moved in," Silas shrugged, chuckling.

Zayn took a deep, relieving breath. "Do you feel as relieved as I am to have someone else to talk to about your extracurricular activities?" It was as if he felt the weight lifted off his shoulders, sharing his secret.

"I was nervous at first, but you're right. I do feel like a weight has been lifted. I'm no longer having to hide who I am from *everyone*."

"How would you feel about meeting up once a week to talk about what we are working on?"

"We should do that. How do you feel about Wednesday evenings?" Silas inquired.

"Wednesdays are perfect. It's just going to be the two of us, right?" Zayn asked.

"Unless you find, or know of, another person who engages in the same activities, it will be just the two of us."

"Yeah, what are the odds that we will find someone else who enjoys the same hobby?"

"Well, your mother will be safe here. I was thinking about inviting the guys over, but I don't know if Derik will want to see me right now."

"Would that have something to do with the fact that he came over last night, then left in a huff this morning?"

"You could tell that he was upset when he left this morning?" Silas asked.

"He was mumbling angrily and sped off down the street," Zayn informed.

"Last night I was stalking, but I began feeling differently about my target. I just needed a release and knew that Derik would come over and help me with that. Unfortunately, I informed him this morning that it didn't mean we were in a relationship. He was pretty upset and left."

"You obviously care for him. Maybe you should try a relationship with him. Derik seems like a great guy."

"I do care about him. That's why I don't want to start a relationship with him. I'm not a cheater."

"What does cheating have to do with it?"

"I strangle my targets during sex. I would be cheating on him. That would cause me to feel guilty. The only way I could confess my infidelity to him would be to give up what I was actually doing with the other man."

"Not necessarily. You could always change the place where you engage in the activity, as well as where you dispose of them."

"Well first, bringing them here contains any evidence that could connect me to a crime. Second, you would be surprised at how great a decomposing body is at fertilizing the flowers," Silas informed.

"Aren't you afraid that someone might notice you bringing someone home that is never seen again?" Zayn inquired.

"No. If anyone asks about the man I brought home, I just say when I woke up, he was gone."

"Have you ever been caught?"

"No. I always make sure that I bring them here so I don't have to worry about disposing of their car. I have perfected the disposal over the years. I know how to get away with it, without getting caught. How about you?"

"I dismember the body and dispose of the parts in different areas. By the time the body parts are discovered, they are decomposed and found by different police departments. Unless they communicate, they won't connect the parts to being the same person."

"That's smart. Is that what you did with your dad?" Silas asked.

"The best part about that, his body hasn't been found. My mother and everyone else thinks he is a fugitive on the run. I'm okay with my mother thinking that I'm keeping her safe from him," Zayn informed.

Twelve

A couple of weeks later, Silas and Zayn were sitting on Zayn's driveway. A nice breeze blew past Jaxon's house and wafted the smell of decay in their direction. The breeze was cooling in the ninety degree still heat, but the rancid stench emanating from Jaxon's house was intriguing to the others. They both recognized it as the scent of decomposition.

Silas and Zayn made eye contact, stood and headed over to Jaxon's house. They had a feeling he was probably in his back yard tending to his manure pile, so they went through the gate and headed toward the far back where Jaxon kept his fertilizer stock.

"Jaxon, what is that awful stench?" Zayn asked, noticing him near one pile with a pitch fork.

"Pig shit. Helps grass grow thicker and gives flowers more vibrant colors," Jaxon answered, as he stabbed the pitch fork into the pile and turned to face his neighbors.

"It smells like the decomposition of flesh," Silas told him, waving his hand back and forth in front of his nose.

"Oh... uh...there might have been a little pig flesh mixed into the shipment. The smell only lasts a few days as the flesh breaks down. I wasn't expecting the breeze today," Jaxon explained, trying to divert their thoughts.

Silas spotted what looked like a human finger sticking out of the side of the manure pile. He walked over to get a closer look and noticed what he knew to be the ridges of a fingerprint. He reached out and pulled on the finger. The digit emerged only for Silas to realize there were three others and a thumb still attached to the hand.

"What the hell is this?" Silas asked, holding the severed hand up to eye level, raising his eyebrows.

"This stuff comes from all over. I get it cheap and don't ask questions. I assume most of the chunks are pig parts," Jaxon said, nervously knowing that swine flesh is closest to human flesh.

"How about you come over to my house for a drink and we can discuss your disposal method," Silas said, tossing the hand back into the pile.

As Silas and Zayn walked away, Jaxon quickly pushed the extremity back into the fertilizer mixture with the end of the wooden handle of the pitch fork, in order to hide it. Jaxon was nervous that his neighbors might call the police, so he tried to catch up with them before they were able to get inside Silas' house.

"Wait up, guys," Jaxon said, with a defeated tone.

"Come on in. We need to talk," Zayn told Jaxon.

The three men entered Silas' house and walked back to his dining room. Zayn and Jaxon sat down at the table as Silas retrieved three beers from his refrigerator, then joined his neighbors.

"So, you have a secret," Zayn said to Jaxon.

"Look, don't call the cops. I'll tell you everything," Jaxon pleaded, fiddling with the beer bottle on the table in front of him.

"Call the cops? Who said we were going to call the cops? It seems that the three of us all engage in the same extracurricular activities," Silas informed Jaxon.

"Wait, what? What kind of extracurricular activities are you talking about?" Jaxon asked, puzzled.

"Are you going to say that you don't know how that hand got in your fertilizer pile?" Zayn wondered.

"I mean...I know how it got there, but I didn't do anything," Jaxon lied, playing with his hands and shrugging his shoulders.

"Okay, listen..." Silas began, turning toward Zayn.

Zayn began telling Jaxon his story. Jaxon seemed shocked at first, but when Silas told Jaxon his story,

Jaxon was relieved. He always felt as though his secret was a burden on him, but after hearing their stories, he felt as though he had finally found friends he could keep for life.

The men knew they were drawn to complete their rituals, but there was always the fear of being caught. No matter how careful they were not to be noticed, or leave any evidence behind, there was always the worry of not slipping and revealing what their hobbies were.

"What are the odds that there are three serial killers living on the same street?" Jaxon inquired.

"Well, now it's your turn. What's your story?" Zayn wanted to know.

"Well, you know how I had initially started experimenting with small animals? I was trying to find the right combination of chemicals in order to be sure it would work on the human body. At first it was just dissection and morbid curiosity. That was until I decided to mow the neighbors lawns for some extra money. At that point it became a business decision. Once I had moved on to rabbits, raccoons and opossums I realized the decomposition was an advantage to the flourishing of my customers yards.

"Eventually their bodies weren't decomposing fast enough, so I had moved on to small pigs. Like I said before, their skin has the closest texture and decomposition time as humans. I wanted to find the right mixture of drain cleaner and heavy duty carbon remover, so I could start mixing the carcasses I truly had the passion to dissect. Once I got the mixture correct, in a couple of days, the pig remains would be practically liquified.

"When I turned twenty-two I wanted to be sure it would have the same effect on a human body. It was then I went downtown where the homeless sleep. I found an old guy who looked like he had been on the streets for decades and asked if he wanted a home cooked meal and a warm bed to sleep in. He was just happy to have someone talk to him.

"He packed up his tent and put his stuff in the trunk of my car. I took him back to my house, let him take a shower while I made him drain cleaner spaghetti with heavy duty carbon remover meatballs. Initially, he was wary about the meal, stating that it smelled weird. The chemicals gave off an odor to the food. At first I didn't think he would eat it, but once I reassured him that it was the smell of the meatballs because they were soy and not real beef, he just shrugged, then devoured the contents of the plate.

"After his last bite, he placed the fork down on the plate and leaned back in the chair. I then showed him to my guest room and waited until morning to check on him. He was on the floor with foam coming out of his mouth and he was dead. I took his body out to my garage and cut it open. I started by scooping out his organs, then poured more of the mixture inside the shell.

"I dismembered the body and injected the mixture into the limbs and head. I tossed the pieces into a wheel barrow and waited a couple of days before I took it out to my fertilizer pile. I mixed the corpse into the dirt, then checked on it the day after. The flesh was falling off the bone and practically melting.

"The more corpses I added, the less manure I needed. I started scattering the fertilizer around at my clients' homes and buried any chunks that hadn't deteriorated at that point. I'm not a total psychopath. The only people I pick up are the homeless, drug addled prostitutes and every so often, a runaway that I find hitchhiking on the side of the road. I offer them a room to sleep in for the night and feed them a home cooked meal. The runaways I keep around until I find out if they have a family that might be looking for them. If they do, I let them go. If they don't, I feed them their last meal," Jaxon explained, nonchalantly.

"Do you hold the runaways hostage, or how does that work?" Zayn wondered.

"Not hostage; I just feed and house them. If they have a family that may look for them if they go missing, after a week I give them a care package and send them on their way. If they don't have any family, I feed them their last meal and they end up in my compost pile," Jaxon stated, matter-of-factly.

"And the others?" Zayn asked.

"No one cares if a homeless person, or a prostitute goes missing. Ninety nine percent of the time, they aren't even reported missing because those types of people don't trust the police," Jaxon said, shrugging.

"Oh thank goodness. Another serial killer who doesn't give a shit if their victims are good people, or not. Now I don't feel like such a total asshole," Silas said.

Zayn and Jaxon laughed, as Silas went to the refrigerator for more beer.

Thirteen

Every Wednesday night Silas, Zayn and Jaxon would rotate with which home they would meet. They would sit around the table and talk about their latest targets. After three months of regular weekly meetings, Silas was the only one of the three who hadn't eliminated his target. Zayn and Jaxon had claimed the lives of two victims each and Silas was feeling the effects of the need.

"I need to get rid of this guy, soon," Silas said, rubbing his forehead.

"Have you talked to him yet?" Jaxon asked.

"I approached him once, just to make sure he was into guys, but I haven't been able to get him to leave with me," Silas informed.

"Let's go get some fresh air," Zayn suggested.

The three men grabbed their beers and packed a few more into a cooler and headed out to sit on Jaxon's driveway. While they were out there, Evander came home with a date. She was a pretty little blonde girl who seemed slightly intoxicated.

"I hope he doesn't plan on taking advantage of that girl," Zayn said.

"We can always hang out here and find out what happens," Silas proposed.

They sat on Jaxon's driveway, drinking beer, waiting for the girl to re-emerge. After a couple of hours, Jaxon mentioned a black vehicle that had parked down the street shortly after Evander pulled up.

"Do you think it's a cop?" Silas asked.

"Why would there be a cop on the street? Oh shit, do you think they know what we have done?" Zayn wondered.

"Zayn, I think you're drunk," Jaxon laughed.

"I think you're right. I could be drunk," Zayn said, opening his eyes as wide as he could.

"Are you sure the car pulled up after Evander and it wasn't already there before we came out? I only remember seeing the headlights of Evander's truck," Silas said.

"I'm positive it pulled up shortly after Evander because I thought it was weird when it turned down the street and parked without its lights on," Jaxon mentioned.

When the sun began to peek over the horizon, the black car started up and backed around the corner, as Evander came out of his house, alone and left in his truck.

"Where is the girl?" Jaxon asked, as he came out of his house with three cups of coffee.

"Maybe he's going to get breakfast?" Silas suggested.

"Maybe he killed her?" Zayn said.

"If he did, wouldn't we have heard her scream?" Jaxon inquired.

"Not if he sound proofed his garage," Silas informed, remembering all the construction noise they heard coming from Evander's home.

"We should go over and check it out, just to make sure she is okay," Jaxon said.

"How about we wait a little while to see if he comes back with breakfast before we get suspicious. I mean, it's already strange that three serial killers live on the same street. What are the odds there are four?" Zayn said.

"It's definitely an anomaly," Silas mentioned.

"You're right," Jaxon agreed, nodding. "What happened to the black car?"

"While you were inside getting coffee, it backed up around the corner," Silas said, sipping his coffee.

"But it's gone now. Must be whoever is driving the black car, is following Evander," Jaxon assumed.

"Well that's a relief," Zayn said.

"Why is it a relief?" Silas asked.

"Because that means if it is a cop, they weren't looking at us," Zayn said, taking a deep breath.

"Zayn, I think you're still drunk," Jaxon told him.

"I think I am too," Zayn admitted.

They sat around for another couple of hours, drinking coffee, waiting for Evander to come home. When he still hadn't arrived and the girl hadn't come out of the house, they debated on whether to go check on the girl, or just go to sleep for a little while.

"Did y'all see the news story about the dead women?" Silas asked.

"I saw that. The police believe that they were all killed by the same person. They weren't prostitutes, so we know it wasn't Jaxon," Zayn said.

"Hey, I don't just dump my victims out in the open. I actually use their decomposing bodies in order to make something else look good," Jaxon defended.

"I wasn't mentioning it to accuse Jaxon; I wanted your opinion as to whether you agree that possibly Evander was the one who killed these girls. They were all young women and they have the same look," Silas mentioned.

"I never thought about that. To top it off, the girl who went into Evander's house last night, she looks similar to the dead girls," Zayn said, leaning forward in his chair.

"Exactly and that could be the reason the cop is following him. Most likely he is already being suspected," Silas told them.

"That makes sense. The cop showed up last night and pointed his vehicle at Evander's home for a straight line of sight. Then he left this morning and followed Evander as he left," Jaxon said, yawning.

They had been up all night spying on Evander and the caffeine in their coffee was no longer able to overpower the fatigue they were beginning to feel.

"This coffee is not keeping me awake anymore. I might doze off right here," Zayn said. "But on the bright side, I don't think I'm drunk anymore."

"If I get up and start moving around, I might be okay," Silas informed. "And I think it's a good thing you're not drunk anymore."

"I think we should peek in his windows, just to be

sure," Jaxon suggested, yawning.

"If she is dead in his garage, the garage doesn't have any windows. How would we know?" Zayn asked.

"She won't be seen in the house. That's how we would know. Come on," Silas said.

They stood up, stretched and slowly walked toward Evander's home. Zayn went through the gate into the backyard, as Jaxon and Silas each picked a side of the house. They began peering into the windows, maneuvering in order to see between the slats in the blinds and the separations in the curtains, but neither one of them saw the woman. The house was empty and they were sure she hadn't left.

"How about we go lay down and get some sleep. I will set up my proximity alarm to go off when he gets home and I will inform y'all when he has arrived," Jaxon proposed.

"Proximity alarm? What's that?" Silas asked.

"I don't want anyone poking around on my property, so I have sensors all the way around my yard. If anyone walks past the sensors, it sends a signal to the app on my phone. When I open the app, it triggers the cameras and I can see who set off the alarm," Jaxon explained.

"Shit, I need that. Can you set me up with something like that?" Silas inquired.

"Can we talk about this later? I don't know how much longer I'm going to be able to hold this upright position," Jaxon asked, yawning.

"Sounds good to me," Zayn said, stretching and yawning.

"I'm good with that," Silas said, blinking slowly as his eyelids were beginning to feel heavy.

The three men went their separate ways as Jaxon turned several of his motion sensor alarms from his driveway and aimed them at Evander's driveway. Silas went inside his home, showered, then laid down on his bed for a quick nap.

Jaxon had barely dozed off when he was awoken by the alert from his alarm. He immediately sent a text to both Silas and Zayn, who met him outside within minutes. They were lucky enough to approach Evander as he was exiting his vehicle.

"Hey, uh, Evander. How was your date last night?" Jaxon engaged a conversation.

"Fine, why?" Evander asked, irritated.

"Well, we figured it must have been good since she hasn't left yet," Zayn accused.

"Oh, yeah," Evander laughed, nervously.

"So, are you going to keep us guessing, or are you going to tell us what really happened?" Silas asked.

"I don't know what you are talking about," Evander said, heading toward his front door in order to avoid having a conversation with his neighbors.

The men surrounded Evander to keep him from going inside. He turned around looking at each one of them before sitting down on his driveway in the middle of the circle of the three men. He placed his elbows on his bent knees and lowered his head. At first he thought he was about to get his ass kicked, so he figured if he started on the ground, the other men would go easy on him.

"We have seen the news about several young women who have been murdered and dumped," Silas told Evander.

"So what," Evander responded, with his forehead resting on his knees.

"They all look like the woman that you brought home with you last night," Jaxon mentioned.

"We just want to know if you are one of us," Zayn inquired.

"Wait, what?" Evander questioned, looking up at the men towering over him.

"That's right. Now tell us what really happened last night," Silas urged.

"I brought home a sex toy last night. That's all she was to me. Nothing else happened," Evander lied.

"Oh really. So you brought her home, had sex with her and now she's just hanging out in your house?" Silas inquired.

"No, she left this morning," Evander said.

"That's not true. We have been watching your house all night and most of the morning. We saw her arrive with you, but she is still inside your house," Zayn said.

"You haven't been out here the whole time. She left when y'all went inside," Evander said, sounding as though he was going to cry.

"She didn't leave with you, so who picked her up?" Jaxon asked.

"Wait, okay she's still inside," Evander said, placing his hands on his knees.

"So we know you have already lied. Are you going to tell us what actually happened to her, or are we going to flag down the cop that has been following you?" Silas said, moving to the side so Evander could see the car that was parked, trying to hide, around the corner.

"Okay, but at least come inside," Evander said, standing up and squeezing between Zayn and Jaxon, making his way toward his front door. "I know that car has been following me. He's been around for about a month, but just recently he started following me home."

"I knew that car was following *him*," Zayn said, bumping Silas with his elbow.

"Technically, last night you thought the car was there to watch *us*," Jaxon corrected.

"I was drunk and paranoid last night," Zayn said,

shrugging.

They followed Evander into his house. He led them to his garage and opened the door. Even though Jaxon, Zayn and Silas had done some pretty gruesome things to their victims, they weren't quite prepared for what they saw.

Fourteen

In the center of the room was a metal table. It was similar to one that would be in a morgue. On that table was the young woman Evander had brought home the night before, naked. He had cut her open and had a bowl next to her body that was full of her internal organs. Internal bodily fluid was draining down the reservoir channel along the edges of the table, through a drain at her feet and into a bucket placed on the floor.

"What happened in here?" Silas asked, as he admired the blood covered, sharp implements lined across a counter along the side wall.

"Well, I got what I wanted out of her first. Once we were finished and we were still naked, I brought her in here and told her I had a fantasy. I tied her arms up over her head and attached it to the bar on that end, then tied up her feet and attached that to the bar on the other end. It started sexual and she was loving it. That was until I pulled out the knife and made the first incision," Evander explained.

"She didn't scream?" Zayn inquired.

"I made sure this room was completely sound proof for specifically what happened last night with the three of you outside all night. I wanted to make sure I wouldn't get caught each time I brought home a dissection project," Evander continued.

"So, why is that car following you?" Jaxon asked.

"I don't know. I would assume they have suspicion, but not enough evidence to charge me with anything, so they sent out someone to try to find something on me," Evander assumed.

"Well, if you are being scrutinized by a police detective, that puts the three of us on their radar as well," Silas told him.

"Why would the police give a shit about you three?" Evander inquired.

Beginning with Zayn, the men told Evander about their experience with their first victims and how they dispose of the bodies in order to ensure anonymity. Zayn was the most moral out of the others, due to the fact that he was, in a way, sacrificing the few, to save the many. Jaxon shared before Silas and Evander seemed excited by Silas.

"Hell yeah. That's the best way to do it. Gotta get the release before they go, right?" Evander said, excited.

"What about you? How did you get started?" Zayn asked.

"It truly started when I was thirteen. Once the hormones started flowing through my body, I became obsessed with girls. Unfortunately, girls were never interested in me. It caused me to have a short temper. When I was seventeen and went on vacation with my parents and my brother, I met a girl who was staying in the same hotel.

"I tried to get her attention, but she told me to leave her alone. I got angry, knocked her out, dragged her into the pool maintenance room and stabbed her repeatedly with a screwdriver I found. I left her dead body in the pool maintenance room, jumped into the pool to try to clean off the blood and headed back to the room I shared with my brother." Evander gave them the abridged version of events of his first kill.

"No one noticed you talking to the girl?" Jaxon inquired.

"I wasn't memorable enough for anyone to know that I was pursuing her, so I wasn't even suspected. I got away with it and it became a sexual release for me to kill the girls who rejected me after they showed me the slightest amount of attention.

"It gave me a rush to know that I had gotten away with murder each time one of my victims was found. I began posing each one of the bodies in different ways, then waited for the news to report about the discovery.

"At some point I started to cut open my victims and remove the organs. As you can see, I leave the body open for a while to ensure all of the blood and liquids drain. Now whenever they are discovered, their insides have been replaced with rocks," Evander told them.

"That's why you are being tailed. You have created a signature to your kills and the police have caught on. Most likely they have spoken to your friends and that's why you are suspected. They just have to prove that it actually is you, without spooking you into leaving town," Silas said, rolling his eyes.

"When I left this morning, I went to the hardware store and picked up several bags of rocks. That car followed me all the way there and back." Evander began pacing back and forth, looking down at the floor.

"Well, if you are willing to help me, I'm willing to help you," Jaxon told him.

"How?" Evander asked.

"First, forget about the rocks. Second, let's cut this

bitch up. We can fill her with my chemical mixture and soak the limbs in the barrels before throwing her into my fertilizer pile. That way, the body is disposed of and you don't have to worry about it being found," Jaxon offered.

"I don't know you and at this point, I don't trust you. So, I think I am just going to continue doing what I do and maybe someday you'll see that my disposal method is better," Evander told him.

"Apparently not if you're being followed by the police," Silas said, lifting his arms over his head and allowing them to fall down by his sides.

"I don't even know if that car has a cop in it. Maybe I have a stalker," Evander said, condescendingly.

"If you don't trust us, then why did you tell us about your little hobby?" Jaxon said, crossing his arms over his chest.

"I felt inclined to tell you, since you felt inclined to share with me," Evander retorted, mirroring Jaxon's stance.

"Well, if you ever want to, the three of us meet

every Wednesday to discuss the target we have chosen. You are more than welcome to join us," Silas invited him, trying to cut the tension.

"Yeah, maybe. I'm going to finish up here and clean up the mess. Maybe I'll see you guys later," Evander said, trying to rush his neighbors out.

Silas, Zayn and Jaxon left Evander's home and walked over to Zayn's house to check on Edna. Silas and Jaxon sat in the living room as Zayn went to Edna's room.

"What are the chances that Evander will probably join us for our Wednesday meetings?" Jaxon asked Silas.

"Who knows. I think that once he realizes he's not alone, he might show up," Silas theorized.

Zayn returned to the living room, pushing Edna in her wheelchair to join the group. Before Zayn could sit down, there was a knock on the front door.

"I guess it didn't take long for Evander to decide we were cool enough to hang with." Silas laughed, as Zayn walked over to answer the door.

Standing on the front porch was a bald, six foot

tall man wearing a white dress shirt, grey slacks and had a police detective badge hanging around his neck. The man not only had a pistol in a holster clipped to his belt, he also had a taser.

"Hello officer. How can I help you?" Zayn greeted the guest.

"I'm Detective George Mage. Can I come in and ask you guys some questions about your neighbor?" the man requested.

"Sure, come on in, detective," Zayn said, moving to the side in order for Mage to enter the residence.

"Ma'am, gentlemen," the detective acknowledged the others, before sitting down on the only single chair in the living room.

Zayn sat down on the love seat, as Silas and Jaxon were occupying the sofa. Edna leaned back in her wheelchair and propped one of her elbows up on the push handle, as though she was trying to appear intimidating.

"So how much do y'all know about your neighbor?" Mage asked.

"Which neighbor?" Silas asked, strumming his

fingertips against each other and tilting his head.

"Evander Thomson," Mage answered, raising his eyebrows at Silas.

"We just recently met the guy, so we don't know how much help we can be to you." Jaxon answered prematurely, as he picked at the skin on his fingers.

"That's okay. I have some very specific questions. If you genuinely don't know the answer, it's okay to say you don't know," Detective Mage reassured Jaxon.

"My boys here aren't in any trouble, are they detective?" Edna asked, raising her eyebrows.

"No ma'am. Not at all. Now, do you know when Mr. Thomson moved in to that house?" Mage asked, retrieving a small notebook from his shirt pocket.

"He's only been there for about six months," Silas answered.

"Have you ever seen anyone go into the house, but not leave?" Mage asked.

"Well, we don't keep tabs on him, or his house guests. I can't definitively confirm that he is holding anyone hostage," Zayn said, shrugging his shoulders.

"That's not what I meant. Your neighbor is being investigated for murder," Mage informed.

"MURDER!" Edna screeched, leaning forward in her wheelchair. "Arrest him! Get him off our street!"

"It's not that simple, ma'am. At this point it is only speculation. We are looking for witnesses and concrete evidence to prove what we suspect," Mage told her.

"We have never suspected that Evander would have murdered anyone," Silas replied.

"Well, if y'all see anything suspicious, please give me a call," Mage said, as he stood and retrieved a business card from his back pocket.

"We will definitely keep an eye out for you, detective. We do *not* want a murderer living on our street," Edna told Mage, as he headed out of the front door.

"I guess the next time we are outside, relaxing on the driveway, we should probably pay more attention to Evander and what he might be doing over there," Zayn said, trying to comfort his mother.

"Why don't we go out there now, just in case he is doing anything illegal," Jaxon suggested.

"Good, you boys go outside and keep an eye on that murderous psycho," Edna encouraged.

Silas and Jaxon headed outside, while Zayn made sure that his mother was comfortable on the sofa with her favorite television show playing. Once he was sure she was settled in for a few hours, Zayn stepped outside with his neighbors.

"Okay, so Jaxon is on hiatus for a little while, Zayn what are you working on?" Silas asked, as Zayn sat down to join them.

"Evander's truck is gone, for now, so we have a little while to discuss your targets," Jaxon mentioned.

"I'm still gathering information. This guy's wife was cooperative in the beginning, but now she worried that I might make the situation worse and she has retracted some of the initial information. What about you Silas? How are you doing with your target?" Zayn asked.

Before Silas could answer, Evander came driving down the street. The men watched as their neighbor exited his truck, then walked over toward them. Silas, Zayn and Jaxon straightened their posture in their seats as Evander stopped in front of them.

"Hi, did you need something?" Zayn said, indifferent.

"I thought about it and decided I would like to join you guys for your meeting," Evander requested.

"So, have you decided that we could be an asset of information to you?" Zayn asked.

"I guess…I mean…well…never mind. This was a mistake," Evander stammered, turning to walk away.

"No, no. Come back. Silas, continue. Tell us how it's going," Zayn said, standing and heading toward his garage to retrieve a fourth chair.

"I don't know if I'm comfortable talking about this in front of someone who is being investigated by the police," Silas said, as Evander sat down and Zayn returned.

"Silas, this is suppose to be a safe space for us to encourage one another, not for us to tear each other down," Zayn scolded.

"What do you mean I am being investigated by the police?" Evander asked, shifting his eye contact quickly back and forth between the other men.

"The man driving that black car came to talk to us about an hour ago. He says they are trying to gather evidence against you for murder. You stupid mother fucker. You have now put the three of us under that microscope as well," Silas said, standing and tossing an empty beer bottle at Evander.

"I didn't think... uh," Evander began.

"That's right, you didn't think," Silas spat.

"Can we just get over this. Evander knows he fucked up. Maybe now he will put his activity on hold for a little while until the heat cools off. Silas, you were saying," Zayn said.

Fifteen

"**O**kay, so I have been stalking my target for at least six months. By this time, I have normally had my kill and am moving on to the next. I couldn't get him to approach me, so I approached him the last time I went over to his city. I just need to get him to come home with me. I have never had this problem before,"

Silas said, rubbing his face.

"How far is the drive out to your victim?" Zayn asked.

"It's about four hours. I always make sure my targets live far enough, so no one knows who I am and I am never suspected," Silas said.

"What about approaching him and going back to his house instead?" Evander suggested.

"I never leave a body behind," Silas told him.

"Why does it matter?" Evander said, shrugging.

"I can't guarantee that I won't be seen, or have witnesses. If I bring my victims to my house, I have a better chance to not make a mistake and not get caught. If I go to their house, I have to be sure to clean up before I leave and risk leaving evidence behind," Silas informed.

"I guess, but wouldn't it just be easier to go to his house and finish him off?" Evander said, taking a swig of beer.

"Have you ever finished off one of your targets at their house, or do you always bring them to your place?" Zayn inquired.

"Of course not. My residence is the safest place to dissect my targets. I would never cut them up at their house because when they are reported missing there is too much evidence left behind. I always bring them back to my place," Evander said.

"So you see my problem," Silas said, shrugging.

"Do you know where the guy lives?" Evander asked.

"Yes I do, but what does that have to do with my problem?" Silas inquired.

"You could always break into his house and abduct him, then bring him back to your house," Evander suggested.

"I need him to consent to the sexual act," Silas said.

"Wait, you want them to consent to sex, but then you don't ask their permission to strangle them," Evander laughed.

"Okay well, that wasn't helpful. Have you thought about getting him drunk so that he wouldn't even notice you are taking him to your house," Jaxon suggested.

"I have a date with him this weekend. I'm surveilling him at his house for the next couple of days, so I can figure out how many drinks it might take him to get drunk and into my car. I thought about making the suggestion to meet him at his house, but then I figured why would he want to go to my house if we were already at his house. I made reservations at a restaurant and I will be picking him up at his house and driving him there, so he will already be in my car," Silas informed them.

"That sounds like a good idea. Are you going to get him completely hammered so he doesn't realize that y'all are going to your house and not his?" Jaxon replied.

"That's what I was hoping for. He usually has about four beers a night, so the plan was to try to get him to drink a bottle of wine," Silas said, his mood improving.

"This is stupid. All you have to do is offer him some dick and he should be more than willing to go to your house," Evander shouted, standing up.

"First of all, keep your voice down. Secondly, my

targets aren't slutty little girls like yours are. It's a little more complicated to convince a man to go home with you for an intimate evening than it is for some slutty, drunk, white chick. She's willing to do anything once she's drunk," Silas berated Evander.

"Whatever asshole. I bet I could get any guy to come home with me," Evander stated, confidently, shifting his weight to his right side.

"I'd like to see that. I have a few friends you could try that on," Silas suggested.

"I'm not going to hit on your friends. You'd tell them to reject me and I would fail," Evander said, turning to leave.

"Well, if you find a man to come home with you, let us know. I'd love to get some tips if you succeed," Silas smirked.

"Fuck you guys, I'm going home to deal with some business," Evander huffed, heading back across the street.

"Let us know if you need any help hiding that girl's body," Jaxon shouted, as Evander slammed the front door behind him.

The three guys laughed and drank a couple more beers before parting ways for the night. Silas stayed up late planning out his date, along with the extras. He really needed his release, but wanted to get it from strangling a guy. He still felt bad about his exchange with Derik.

Derik was a really great guy and maybe someday Silas could see the two of them getting married, but it just wasn't the right time in Silas' life to take on a relationship. Derik was boyfriend/husband material, not just a conquest.

The one thing Silas could rely on was that Derik was waiting for him to be ready for a relationship. Derik wasn't dating anyone and never did. If Silas was ever built up, he knew Derik would come over with just a little flirting and coercing.

Sixteen

When the night came for Silas to meet up with Stuart, he made sure he was freshly shaven, all over his body. He put on a nice pair of black slacks and a light blue collared shirt. He had been looking forward to this night since he had the meeting with Zayn and Jaxon and they were able to help him with his plan.

Evander was still young and acted like he knew every-thing.

As he headed out, Zayn and Jaxon were waiting for him by his vehicle. He greeted them, as they greet-ed him.

"Now, don't get him too drunk, just get him tipsy. If he is too drunk he might be less cooperative and possibly belligerent," Jaxon informed Silas.

"Right. And make sure that he drinks more of the wine than you do. That could potentially get him to your house easier, but you don't want him passing out before the finale," Zayn said.

"Okay guys. Hey, where's Evander?" Silas in-quired, noticing the empty driveway next door.

"He left about an hour ago. Maybe he has another victim he is scouting, or possibly finally dumping the body of the girl from his garage," Zayn said.

"Maybe he just went to work. He does work in retail and has a random work schedule," Jaxon retort-ed.

"Whatever, I just thought that maybe he would have changed his view and decide to be a part of the group," Silas said, shrugging.

"Have fun and let me know if you need help with disposal of the body," Jaxon offered.

"Will do. Thank you," Silas said, opening his car door.

As Silas drove the four hours to meet his mark, he thought about what Evander said about just doing it at the victim's house. He knew that wouldn't be an option. He didn't want to leave any evidence behind that could suggest that a murder took place in the house.

It would also be difficult to leave the house with a body without being noticed. He knew it was a bad idea, but couldn't help thinking that it could potentially be easier just to leave the body behind. The only downside would be that he likes to go bareback and he would leave too much DNA behind. Plus, all supplies were already setup at Silas' house.

When Silas pulled up to the house, he thought it seemed a little dark inside, but blew it off as ambiance. He parked the car on the street, in order to make an easy getaway with the passenger side facing the house. Before opening his car door, Silas looked around, just to make sure there weren't any witnesses around who could pick him out of a lineup.

Slowly, he exited the vehicle, checked himself out in the reflection on his window, then headed up to the front door. He gently knocked at first. When he didn't get an answer after a few moments, he knocked a little harder thinking his target was probably in the house somewhere he may not have been able to hear the light rapping.

When no one came to the door after ten minutes, Silas rang the doorbell and tried peering into the front windows. He found a split in the curtain from the bay window that looked into the living room. On the floor, in the middle of the room, surrounded by a pool of blood, was Stuart...dead.

Stuart was naked and sprawled out in a crude pose, lying face down with his rear end propped up in the air. Silas had an idea of who could have stollen his target, but with the distance, he wasn't sure. Quickly walking back to his car, Silas slid in behind the steering wheel. He sat in the driver's seat, slamming the palms of his hands against the steering wheel. He gripped the wheel and yanked on it, while screaming and yelling, "FUCK". Someone beat him to it; someone else killed his target.

He started the engine, shifted the vehicle into drive and drove away, heading back to his home. He didn't understand how this could have happened. He wondered if maybe someone else wanted to kill Stuart.

Frustrated, Silas managed to make it home in just a little over an hour. He whipped his vehicle onto the driveway of his home and shoved it into park. Zayn and Jaxon were relaxing on Jaxon's driveway and came walking over when Silas opened the door to his vehicle.

"Mother Fucker!" Silas yelled, as his neighbors approached.

"You're back early. What happened?" Zayn asked, as Silas stood up.

"Someone beat me to it," Silas said, dumbfounded.

"What do you mean, someone beat you to it?" Jaxon inquired.

"My target was already dead when I got there. Luckily, it was dark when I arrived, so no one noticed me. Who would have done this?" Silas said.

"Do you think there is a possibility of another serial killer living in his city?" Zayn stated.

"I think we have a traitor among us," Silas said, matter-of-factly.

"A traitor?" Jaxon asked.

"I believe it was one of the four of us. There is someone that I told about my target who decided to take that from me," Silas said, narrowing his eyes.

"Do you really think we would do that?" Zayn inquired.

"Well, not necessarily you two, but someone did," Silas said.

"You're thinking Evander?" Jaxon wondered.

"I can only speculate, but he knew when I was going over there, he was gone hours before I left and he is home now. Isn't it possible that he could have gone over there and killed my target before I could?" Silas stated.

"What are you going to do? Are you going to confront him?" Jaxon wanted to know.

"I need a plan to find out if he really did," Silas said.

"Let's go inside. I can help you with that," Jaxon said, trying to lure Silas toward his house.

The three men walked over to Jaxon's house and went inside, sitting around the dining room table. Jaxon retrieved a few beers from the refrigerator and they began to plan how to get Evander to admit to the treason.

Seventeen

"**H**e is so vain, he may just come right out and admit it. Why don't we go over there and just ask him?" Zayn said.

"Instead of just going over there and accusing him, why don't we invite him over and see if he has any advice on how to handle the situation," Jaxon suggested.

"I like that idea. Let's go," Silas said, taking a huge swig of his beer, then slamming the bottle down on the table.

The men headed over to Evander's home and Jaxon pounded on the door with his fist. It didn't take long for their neighbor to answer.

"Hey guys. What's going on?" Evander asked.

"We have a problem. You wouldn't mind coming over to Silas' house to help us out, would you?" Jaxon stated.

"How about y'all come in," Evander said, moving to the side of the open door and allowing his neighbors to enter his domicile.

The men walked in and sat down on the sofa in the living room, as Evander closed the door. He joined his neighbors and waited for one of them to speak first. When no one spoke, Evander wondered what was going on. His neighbors were just glaring at him.

"What's the problem?" Evander wanted to know.

"When I went to meet up with my target, he had already been killed; sloppily I might add, by someone else. I needed my kill and don't know what to do now," Silas said, as defeated as possible.

"Well, I don't know about how sloppy it was done, but it can't be that big of a deal," Evander said.

"No, it was awful. There was blood everywhere and he was left in the middle of the floor in his living room. I need to strangle someone," Silas responded, balling his hands into fists.

"It can't be that bad. We all have our different styles, who's to say that this other guy doesn't have a different style from the four of us?" Evander attempted to defend.

"I don't think that the person who killed him is a professional. I think he is an amateur and it also could have been a robbery gone wrong," Zayn said.

"It could have also been his first kill," Jaxon included.

"Maybe it was a woman," Silas chimed in.

"Amateur? His first kill? A woman? Is it fair to say that?" Evander inquired.

"With the mess that was left, it had to have been either the victim must have surprised someone trying to rob his home, the killer was just walking past the house and thought about Stuart as a victim of opportunity, or some woman who thought she was going to get lucky just to find out he was gay. There is no way it was planned out properly," Silas responded.

Evander became visibly upset. "Just because someone does something differently than you, doesn't mean they were caught off guard, or it was a victim of opportunity. Who's to say the killer didn't wait around for the guy to come home?"

"Why are you taking this so personally?" Silas asked, even though Evander's reaction had already revealed what he suspected.

"I wouldn't want to be trashed behind my back for my kill style. It's not fair that you would do that to someone else," Evander spat.

"If it wasn't you, I don't understand why you would be so defensive," Zayn said.

"Maybe it was. I went in there, waited for the guy to come home and took him out," Evander admitted.

"Why would you *do* that?" Jaxon asked.

"I just wanted to prove to you that killing him at

home and just leaving the body there, wouldn't necessarily point law enforcement in your direction. They won't be able to solve the murder. I made sure I didn't leave any evidence behind," Evander defended himself.

"That's beside the point. What you did was take a target away from a potential ally. You have now made three enemies that are no longer willing to help you. If we are approached by that detective again with questions about this specific murder, we will throw you under the bus. You are no longer protected. Good luck not getting caught," Silas said, standing.

Jaxon and Zayn stood as well and the three headed toward the front door to leave. Just as they stepped out of the house, Evander ran over.

"Wait, what does that mean? Are you going to plant evidence to point toward me?" Evander asked, concerned.

"I don't think we need to plant the evidence. I'm sure you have dug your own grave fucking with my shit. Don't be surprised if we don't acknowledge you anymore. Just keep in mind that we are older and more experienced than you. You should be worried," Silas warned.

As the neighbors walked away from Evander's house, the three of them were already hatching a plan. It was a plan that would either ruin, or end Evander's life, depending on what they deemed fit for his betrayal.

"We have to do something about him. Evander can't get away with this," Silas said, as the three guys stopped at the bottom of Evander's driveway.

"It would be worse for me, if I brought home a runaway that I was going to release and Evander came over and killed them. That could get me arrested," Jaxon commented, picking at the skin around his thumbs.

"How do you think it would be for me? These battered women don't know I kill their abusers. If he were to just go over to their house and murder these men in their homes and then their wife comes home, finding them dead on the floor. This is bad for all of us," Zayn said.

The men noticed the black car was again parked at

the end of the street, so they decided to split up and went to their own homes without saying another word to each other. After a couple hours, the men again emerged from their homes to combine their plans, in order to compile the best course of action to deal with the situation at hand.

They chose to sit on Zayn's driveway, since his house was the furthest away from where the detective was parked, watching Evander's house.

"Evander has gone too far. If he stole Silas' target, how long would it be before he stole Jaxon's, or even mine. He needs to be stopped," Zayn said.

Eighteen

The following day, Zayn and Jaxon walked over to Silas' house to discuss the plan to get back at Evander. They were not going to allow him to get away with stealing a target. Their conversation was put on hold when Detective Mage blocked Silas from closing his front door after Zayn and Jaxon had stepped over the threshold.

"Detective, what can we do for you?" Silas asked, allowing Mage to enter.

"I have a few photos I would like you guys to look at. Would you be willing to help me out again?" Mage asked.

"Sure, let's go into my dining room, so we can use the table," Silas suggested, as he closed the door.

Mage lined up four photos on the table. "Have any of you seen either of these young women?"

"The first three I can't be sure, but the last one, I know for sure I have seen her," Zayn said.

"The second girl, I'm sure had been passed out on my lawn several months ago, but the last girl, I saw her walk into Evander's home a few days ago," Silas told him.

"I can affirm that the last girl had been seen going into Evander's home," Jaxon confirmed.

"Okay, each of you said you saw this young woman enter the residence, but have any of you seen her leave?" Mage asked.

"We don't exactly get along with Evander. More

times than not, we aren't actually paying attention to what goes on at his house," Silas said, rolling his eyes.

"You know I have been watching his house for several days. I saw y'all come out of his house last night. When y'all were in there, did you see any signs that a murder may have taken place in there?" Mage inquired.

"If you're asking if there was blood splattered all over the walls and body parts laying around, no it did not appear as if he had killed anyone inside his house." Zayn chose his words very carefully.

"Is there anyway that you guys could possibly give me a call if you see anything suspicious?" Mage requested.

"We have jobs," Silas told him, irritated.

Silas wanted to kill Evander for what he had done. He didn't want to babysit him in order to report back to a police detective. Zayn was nudging Silas with his elbow and widening his eyes, as if he was trying to tell Silas something.

"You know detective, we would be happy to keep an eye on our neighbor for you. The three of us practically work from home, so it shouldn't be too difficult for us," Zayn agreed.

"That little shit ruined a very important moment for me! I would rather pretend he didn't exist!" Silas yelled.

"What exactly did he ruin for you?" Mage wanted to know.

"Nothing, he's just being overdramatic," Jaxon said, backhanding Silas' arm.

"Did he take a girl from you?" Mage asked.

"Detective, I would pursue you, before I pursued a female. Do you get where I'm going with that?" Silas replied, walking over to his living room and plopping down on the sofa.

"Okay, well if you guys see anything within the next few days, please give me a call," Mage requested, as he collected the photos and headed out.

As soon as the front door was closed, Zayn quickly walked over to engage the dead bolt and look out the peep hole. He wanted to make sure the detective was gone and he couldn't surprise them by just walking in.

"What the hell was that?" Jaxon said, joining Silas in the living room.

"Yeah, are you trying to give yourself away," Zayn scoffed, sitting down next to Silas.

"Why did you agree to watch the traitor?" Silas asked.

"Because, if we are watching him for the detective, that means that the detective isn't watching us," Zayn revealed.

"That's smart. So you think we could eliminate Evander before the detective comes back?" Silas asked, sitting up on the edge of his seat.

"That is a possibility, but I think we should put all our ideas together and come up with the ultimate plan," Jaxon said, placing a one inch binder that he had been clutching onto on the coffee table.

"Did you do research on Evander?" Zayn asked.

"I wanted to make sure we had as much information about the kid, so we could come up with the best course of action," Jaxon replied.

"You are always so organized. That's a great quality to possess in this business," Silas stated.

"It could only be a business if we were getting paid for it," Zayn laughed.

"Now, this kid is a sloppy killer. He tends to choose the girls in his friend circle. According to police records, he has been questioned about the disappearance of several women he has come into contact with on a regular basis. He tends to leave several witnesses behind when he leaves public places with his victims. He has friends who suspect he's not who he says he is and he uses his retail job as a cover," Jaxon began.

"Where does he actually get his money from? I know he said his parents pay the mortgage on that house, but is that even true. Maybe he killed his parents and are using money he stole from them to pay his bills," Zayn inquired.

"According to the records I could find, the house isn't even in his name. His parents purchased it in order to get him away from his little brother. He is kept on the family payroll, but only if he keeps limited contact with his family. There is one arrest record for him that hasn't been completely retracted, whereas the other five have been sealed by the juvenile courts," Jaxon continued.

"What was he arrested for?" Silas asked.

"Apparently, when he was nineteen, he was teaching his brother how to cut open animal carcasses. His parents walked in and overheard him telling his brother that cutting open human bodies are a little easier because our flesh isn't as thick as animal hide. His parents were concerned by this statement and called the police," Jaxon informed.

"So in other words, his parents didn't want him to corrupt his little brother?" Silas said.

"Something like that. From what I found, his parents were worried about him being a little psychotic and figured if he spent some time in jail, or even in a mental hospital, he could potentially turn normal," Jaxon finished.

"What is normal, really," Zayn said, laughing.

"His parents are so naïve," Silas said, rolling his eyes.

"So, what happened?" Zayn asked.

"According to the arrest record, the police questioned him, but didn't have enough evidence to charge him with anything. It's not illegal to teach someone how to cut open animals, nor is it illegal to discuss cutting open humans. Since there wasn't any evidence to prove he had actually committed a crime, he was never charged with anything. They just held him for 72 hours, then let him go home. According to the release, it was mostly to give his parents a break," Jaxon told them.

"That's fucked up. His parents had him arrested and the police didn't do anything to stop him from killing. Sounds like a problem with our justice system," Silas said, leaning back against the sofa.

"But it's a problem that has kept us three out of jail," Zayn pointed out.

"Oh no, what has kept us out of jail is our ability to fake normalcy and our disposal methods. We don't just leave our victims out in the open to be discovered," Silas said.

"That's true," Zayn agreed.

"Have you guys come up with any plan as to how to take care of him? I think we should break into his house and gather evidence to plant at the home of the man he just killed," Jaxon mentioned.

"We aren't B&E experts. Do any of you know how to pick a lock?" Silas asked.

"Fuck picking the lock. We can just break a window and let ourselves in," Jaxon said.

"If we break in, we might as well just kill him," Silas mentioned, shrugging.

"I think we should scare him off until he moves. We don't want him to steal another target," Zayn said.

"We could always just ignore Evander. If we don't tell him about our targets, he won't be able to steal another one," Jaxon suggested.

"Well, it was my target he took from me. I think I should show him exactly what I do when I choose my targets, but not enough to kill him. Once I am done with him, I think we should tie him up, then cut him open, just like he does to his own targets. We can stop, if he can convince us that he is remorseful for the theft and we believe he would never do it again," Silas said, tilting his head back against the sofa and looking up at the ceiling.

"Holy shit, Silas. That sounds like way more fun than what we had planned," Zayn said, smiling from ear to ear.

"Y'all can watch while I fuck and strangle him, or just wait until he passes out," Silas said, lifting his arms and cradling the back of his head in his hands.

"Oh come on, Silas. You don't need to fuck him," Jaxon scoffed.

"Yes, please don't fuck him," Zayn sighed.

"Fine, but you know he has sex with his targets before he cuts them open. I just thought I would repay the favor," Silas told them.

"Yeah, let's keep brainstorming," Jaxon suggested.

"I wonder if Stewart's body has been found," Zayn said.

Silas leaned forward and picked up the remote, turning on his television. "Let's find out."

As he tuned in to the news, Silas recognized the outside of Stewart's home behind the newscaster. "Early this morning, neighbors noticed their one neighbor who never deviated from his normal routine had not emerged from his home. They called the police for a wellness check. That was when the body of thirty year old Stuart Calvert was found nude in the middle of his living room floor, surrounded by a pool of his own blood. Forensics is on scene now gathering evidence. The police have no suspects and at this point don't have any leads. If anyone knows anything, the police are asking you to contact the tip line."

"Well, I guess that answers that. As they collect evidence they may find a suspect," Silas said, muting the television.

"Let's hope they find the right suspect. For now we need to figure out how to take care of the traitor," Zayn suggested.

The three men walked over to the dining room, sat down and began planning the best course of action on how to eliminate Evander.

Nineteen

Once they had agreed upon a plan, Zayn, Jaxon and Silas went through the week as normal. They wanted to go after the enemy when he wasn't expecting it.

Evander had no idea what they were planning, but he tried to stay alert to be prepared. He would wave and be friendly when the guys were sitting out in front of one of their houses, but they never acknowledged him. When nothing happened after a few days, he just lived his life and began ignoring them as well.

At the end of the week, Evander decided that his neighbors had probably chosen not to retaliate. With that, he brought home a new victim. As he pulled into his driveway with the girl, he noticed his neighbors were camped out next door at Silas' house.

"You might want to run little girl. He's planning to kill you," Silas yelled, as Evander opened the passenger door to his vehicle.

"Excuse me?" she asked.

"That man you just came home with is going to kill you and cut your body open," Zayn said.

"What are they talking about?" she asked Evander.

"They are just angry old men. Come on girl," Evander said, encouraging her to go into his house.

"Are you guys serious? Should I leave," the girl asked, walking toward the three men.

"He will cut you open while you are still alive and dissect your body," Silas continued.

"Oh my god. You know what Charlie, I think I'm just going to go. Your neighbors are creepy and I just want to go home," the girl said to Evander.

"He told you his name is Charlie?" Zayn said, as the three men laughed.

"Come on. Just come inside and ignore them," Evander told her.

"No, thank you. I'm just going to walk up to the corner store and call a friend to come get me," she said, heading down the street, away from the cul-de-sac.

"What the fuck dudes?" Evander said, as he approached his neighbors.

"You told her your name is Charlie?" Jaxon asked.

"That's so that if someone reports her as missing, they will tell the police she was last seen with a guy named Charlie Dipole. They will never find me," Evander admitted.

"Well, at least we were able to save that poor girl," Zayn said.

"Why the fuck did you chase her off?" Evander asked.

"You stole my target, so we stole yours," Silas told him, smiling and holding his head up high.

"That's fucked up. You guys are fucked up. I killed that guy because you were acting like a pansy about getting him back to your house. Who cares how you get him back to your house. Just fuck him up at his house and walk away. It was just that easy," Evander said.

"The news stated that Stewart had also been sodomized. That means you fucked him too!" Silas yelled at Evander.

"I just wanted to prove a point," Evander said.

Silas, Zayn and Jaxon stood up and walked toward Evander. As they got closer to him, Evander turned and ran toward his front door. Once the front door was opened, Evander's neighbors rushed into his house and slammed the door behind them. They cornered him in his living room, as Silas grabbed Evander and wrapped his arm around his neck.

"We are going to fuck you up," Zayn told Evander.

Evander struggled under Silas' thick arm, kicking his legs, trying to keep Jaxon and Zayn from getting too close to him. Silas squeezed tighter against Evander's throat to stop the thrashing. Once he was subdued, Jaxon and Zayn removed Evander's clothing. Silas then dragged Evander to the sound proofed garage and body slammed him down on the metal table, ass up.

As Evander gasped to catch his breath, his neighbors tied his hands behind his back and wrapped a rope around his ankles. He struggled under his bindings, but Silas, Jaxon and Zayn made sure he couldn't get away.

"You're lucky my colleagues didn't think that it was a good idea for me to take you out the way I do with my targets. I really wanted to fuck you in the ass until you shit blood. Although, they thought it was more fitting that we dissect you, as you do to your victims," Silas told Evander, as he lightly ran his finger along Evander's exposed ass crack.

Evander clenched his butt cheeks together, in order to avoid the possibility of Silas slipping his finger into the opening. Silas, Jaxon and Zayn each chose a sharp implement and pulled on rubber gloves, as they stood over Evander. Jaxon stood to Evander's left, Zayn stood to the right and Silas was down at Evander's feet.

"Shouldn't we turn him face up, so we can cut him open?" Jaxon suggested.

"I wanted to shove stuff up his ass," Silas said, whining like a toddler.

"Okay, you need to stop thinking about his ass. Let's turn him over," Zayn told them.

The three men grabbed him and forcefully flipped him over on the metal table, knocking the wind out of him. He gasped for air a second time, as they re-situated his bindings and strapped him down to the table.

"This is fucked up. Y'all can't do this," Evander pleaded, after he caught his breath, still struggling under his bindings.

"Sure we can," Silas said, placing the knife he had, just under Evander's scrotum.

"Whoa, whoa! Hold on. Why can't we just work together?" Evander asked, as he stopped struggling.

"We already gave you that option and you decided you didn't want to be a part of the group," Jaxon told

Evander.

"Okay, okay. We can do that," Evander said.

"Too late," Silas told him, as he pressed the knife against Evander's testicles and drew the first blood.

Silas sliced from left to right along the bottom of Evander's scrotum. Evander sucked in hard, then yelled out in pain as he exhaled. Silas pressed his fingers into the cut and pulled up, tearing the skin and rubbing the crimson liquid all over the gloves he was wearing. Smearing blood all over on the inside of Evander's thighs, Silas was playing with their victim at that point.

"No, please stop! Please stop!" Evander screamed.

"We aren't going to stop," Zayn told Evander, placing the knife he had against Evander's shoulder.

Zayn sliced across Evander's pectoral muscle and stopped at the breast bone. Jaxon followed suit and created the same wound as Zayn on the other side of Evander's chest.

"Guys, please! I'm sorry!" Evander yelled.

"You know, I could use his blood as lube," Silas said, as he stroked the blood along Evander's shaft.

"Dude, no. You're not going to fuck him. Call your fuck buddy to come over when we are done to get your rocks off," Zayn said, slicing down Evander's stomach.

"Please...stop," Evander said, between breaths.

"You think I should keep this as a trophy?" Silas said, after removing Evander's penis and holding it up.

"A trophy for what? The smallest dick you've ever seen?" Zayn said, laughing.

"You're right. It's not worth it," Silas said, tossing the phallus over his shoulder.

"Fuck...you...guys," Evander said, through shallow breathing.

"Let me see it," Jaxon told Silas, holding out his hand.

Silas picked it up and handed Evander's penis to Jaxon. Jaxon held it up in front of him, before stuffing it into Evander's mouth and pressing his hand over it as their neighbor choked. Evander began to convulse as he gagged and struggled to breathe, before giving up his fight and releasing one last breath through his nose.

"That's it. Let's cut this fucker up and place him in the manure pile," Jaxon said, peeling open Evander's body.

The three men pulled out Evander's organs and dismembered the body. They piled the pieces up on the table, then went home to clean up.

Twenty

Once they had showered Evander's blood off and changed their clothes, Silas, Zayn and Jaxon met up in front of Evander's house. Before they disposed of his body, they wanted to make sure Detective Mage wasn't sitting in his car down the street. Jaxon brought over a wheel barrow with a layer of fertilizer already piled in, along with a gallon bottle of his chemical mixture and Silas had a bucket for the organs.

They didn't see the vehicle, but just to be sure he hadn't parked around the corner, they set down their disposal items on Evander's driveway and walked down the street. There weren't any vehicles on the road in either direction, so they decided it was safe.

Returning to the house, Jaxon lifted his wheel barrow and headed inside, as Silas picked up his bucket and followed him in, with Zayn right behind him. They entered the garage and began dividing up the parts.

"I'm taking his innards to put in my garden, if you are taking the rest of his body," Silas informed.

"Of course. You can take whatever you need. Also, Zayn, if you would like to dispose of parts of him, you can take pieces as well. We each have our processes and we all took part in this kill," Jaxon said.

"Naw, I'm good. Let's use this fucker as weed and feed," Zayn told them, tossing one of Evander's hands into the wheel barrow.

Jaxon buried each limb under the dirt he brought

and poured his chemical mixture on top. As Jaxon stirred and mixed it all together, Silas dropped Evander's organs into the bucket he brought and used a hand tiller to mix them into an easily pourable liquid. Zayn picked up a cleaner that Evander had sitting on a counter near by and began wiping everything down. The guys didn't leave any evidence behind, to be sure that if Evander's family came by to check on him, they wouldn't find anything amiss.

Zayn went with Jaxon to help mix the contents of the wheel barrow into the fertilizer pile and Silas took the bucket to his back garden. He only had three flower beds so far, but Silas was proud of his garden. He placed a funnel into the opening of his watering can and carefully poured the organ mixture into it.

Once the watering can was filled, Silas placed the bucket on his back patio, near the back door to his house, then picked up the can. Removing the funnel and placing it on the patio table, he walked over to his flower beds and poured the mixture onto the soil.

As he sprinkled the mixture and aerated the dirt, Silas thought about the anger and frustration he felt when he saw that someone had stolen his kill. He was usually a happy person and didn't like the way he felt when he was unable to complete his ritual. As he distributed his neighbor's innards over his garden, he decided he never wanted to feel that angry and vengeful again. It was time for him to change his life.

He wanted to have a normal relationship and he wanted to be with Derik. Once the watering can was empty, he walked over to his patio and hosed out everything that had Evander's DNA. As he rolled the hose back up onto the reel, Zayn and Jaxon entered the yard.

"What happens now?" Jaxon asked.

"Well, we have to figure out something to tell Detective Mage when he asks about Evander," Zayn said.

"Guys, I think it's time for me to retire. I want to have a relationship with Derik and I want to live a normal life. I don't want to have to worry about police detectives spying on me," Silas told them.

"I think we are going to have to hold off for a while as well. With Detective Mage hanging around, we don't want to draw any suspicion to ourselves,"

Jaxon said.

"That's true. Now that Evander is gone, what if the police start looking into us?" Zayn said.

"I was thinking about inviting my friends over for a guys night. You guys want to join us?" Silas suggested.

"That sounds like fun," Zayn said, as they headed through the gate and toward Silas' front yard.

As they were standing on the driveway, the black car pulled up and parked down the street. They waited a few moments to see if Mage would emerge, but no one exited the vehicle. Silas walked toward his front door and the others followed.

"I thought he was done staking out Evander's house," Zayn said, as they sat down in the living room.

"Maybe he just wanted us to watch the house while he was away for a few days. It gave us enough time to eliminate our problem," Jaxon said.

"I agree, but what if some how we created suspicion on us by just talking to him and now he's watching us?" Silas inquired.

"Do you think that could have happened?" Jaxon asked.

"It is possible. Call your friends over, Silas. With Mage watching down the street, we could give the appearance that we are just three normal guys who live a normal life. That could potentially take any suspicion off of us," Zayn told them.

"I agree, but Zayn, you have to bring Edna over," Jaxon said.

"What does Edna have to do with this?" Silas wondered.

"If he brings Edna, a frail old woman, there is no way Mage would suspect that the three of us are a danger to anyone," Jaxon considered.

"That sounds like a good idea. I know my mother would enjoy seeing Frankie again," Zayn informed.

"Perfect. How about you, Jaxon. Do you have anyone special in your life that you would like to invite?" Silas inquired.

"Yeah right. I'm an awkward person all around. I have never pursued a relationship with anyone, ever," Jaxon said.

"Before I call everyone over, I have a question for you guys. If I decide to pursue a relationship with De-rik, should I tell him about my extracurricular activi-ties, or just put it in my past?" Silas inquired.

"It would depend on how much you can trust him. I wouldn't say anything if he is likely to turn you in. Plus, if you plan to stop, there's really no reason to say anything," Jaxon informed.

"You're right. If I am no longer going to engage in autoerotic asphyxiation, it would probably be best not to say anything at all," Silas said, standing.

"Well, while you call your friends over, I'm going to help my mother get ready and hopefully she is up for a night out," Zayn said, heading for the front door.

"Sounds good. Jaxon, do you have anything to do at your house, or would you be willing to help me set up?" Silas asked, as Zayn left.

"I can help you. Just let me know what you need me to do after you arrange the other house guests," Jaxon agreed, as Silas picked up his phone.

Twenty One

"**W**ho's ready to get fucked up and make bad decisions?" Frankie said, as he walked through the front door of Silas' house.

"Hello Frankie," Edna said, from the living room sofa.

"Oh shit. I'm sorry, ma'am. I apologize for my

profane language," Frankie told her, kneeling and bowing his head as if Edna was royalty.

"It's okay Frankie. You are all grown men. I'm sure there are going to be a lot of bad decisions made tonight. I will only be here for a couple of hours, so I don't spoil your fun," Edna informed.

"Girl, you are the life of the party. If you were only allowed to drink, you would probably be one of my good decisions," Frankie said, giggling as he touched her shoulder.

"Oh Frankie, you are my favorite," Edna told him, reaching up to touch his hand.

"If you were a few years younger Edna, I would be all over you," Frankie said.

"If I was a few years younger and had a penis maybe," Edna laughed.

"Zayn, your mother might turn me straight," Frankie said, kicking one leg up behind him.

"Frankie, you are as straight as a corner," Silas told him, walking over to smack his friend on his rear.

"That's true. You're right Edna. You would need a penis to lure me in," Frankie admitted, leaning over the back of the sofa and kissing Edna on her cheek.

"Can we please stop talking about my mother's penis," Zayn requested.

"Now you know I don't really have a penis, son," Edna laughed.

"What fun stuff did you bring us to drink, Frankie?" Silas asked, changing the subject.

"You know I always provide the ingredients for margaritas, bitch," Frankie said, holding up a paper bag full of merchandise.

"Awesome. Let me get out the blender," Silas said, walking over and reaching into a lower cabinet in the kitchen.

"We are planning to get lit tonight. I hope your guest bedroom is free," Barry said, smacking Greg on his rear end, as they entered Silas' house.

"The guest room is free for you to use. Just don't make a mess in there. I don't offer turn down service," Silas told them, laughing.

Frankie mixed up a pitcher full of margaritas and poured glasses for the six men who had already arrived. Derik hadn't shown up at that point and Silas was feeling rejected.

"Since you are unable to partake in spirits Edna, I made yours a virgin on the rocks with strawberry," Frankie said, handing Zayn's mother a special drink.

"It's probably the only virgin in the room," Edna said with a smile.

The room erupted in laughter, as the front door opened. Derik stood in the doorway, brandishing a paper bag of goodies. Silas released a sigh of relief.

"Where's the booze, bitches," Derik practically sang, as he closed the front door.

"The rest of the party has arrived," Frankie said, retrieving another margarita from the kitchen.

"What did you bring?" Silas asked Derik.

"I got snacks," Derik told him.

"Thank you. Would you mind helping me in the kitchen for a moment," Silas requested, hoping to get just a few minutes alone with Derik.

"Sure, I can do that," Derik said, nodding.

Jaxon, Zayn, Frankie, Barry and Greg joined Edna in the living room, as Silas and Derik headed to the kitchen. Silas retrieved several large bowls from the cabinets, as Derik unpacked the grocery bags.

"Look, I really want to apologize for what I said last week. I feel awful. Is there any way that you could forgive me for being an absolute douche?" Silas asked Derik.

"I was hurt that you used me. I thought you liked me, but I was just kidding myself. It's fine Silas, I understand that I was only convenient for your amusement," Derik said, turning toward Silas.

"Derik, please," Silas began, cornering Derik up against the counter. "I really like you and have decided that I want you in my life. That is if you want to be in my life. I haven't been able to stop thinking about you since that night and would really like a chance to make it up to you. I will do anything."

"You would do anything, huh?" Derik said, reaching down and cupping Silas' crotch.

"Don't tease me. I'm really vulnerable here," Silas said, leaning into Derik's grasp.

Derik rubbed his hand up Silas' groin and up his body. He placed his hand on Silas' cheek and kissed him.

"Prove to me that you want a relationship with me and maybe I will forgive you," Derik said, as he pulled away from Silas, then turned and left the kitchen to join the others.

"Did you two make up?" Frankie asked, when Silas appeared with the snacks.

Derik smiled coyly and Silas shifted awkwardly, attempting to hide his excitement. Frankie sat on the sofa next to Edna, leaning his head on her shoulder. Barry and Greg were cuddled up on one cushion of the love seat, as Zayn sat next to Frankie on the sofa and Jaxon occupied the single chair. Derik and Silas smiled at each other, then walked over to cuddle up next to Barry and Greg.

The group sat around laughing and drinking, unaware of what was happening outside in the cul-de-sac.

Twenty Two

Detective Mage was proud of himself for planting the listening device under Silas' dining room table when he had gone over there to talk to the men. They weren't even on his radar until he had heard the vile things they had said.

Once he was sure all of the party guests had arrived, Mage called for backup. He was planning to raid the house and arrest the three killers who had ended Evander's life. There was a dead man found with DNA evidence pointing toward Evander and yet his neighbors took it into their hands to eliminate him.

"What do we have?" the swat team leader asked Mage.

"There are three men in that house who murdered a suspect. We need to be careful, as there are innocent bystanders inside the home as well," Mage began, pulling up photographs of the men on his handheld computer. "We are to only apprehend Zayn Miller, Jaxon Pierce and Silas Graham. Once they have been contained, I will go in and question the others."

"Got it. I will inform my men, then we will assemble to make entry," the swat team leader informed.

Not only had the swat team arrived, the entire cul-de-sac was swarmed with uniformed officers and their vehicles. Mage waited for swat to get into place before the signal to charge the house. Using a battering ram, the door was busted open.

"Down on the ground. Get down on the ground,"

the swat yelled, as they made entry.

Edna sat on the sofa screaming, with her hands in the air, as each one of the men knelt down on the floor with their hands interlocked behind their heads. The swat officers stood over them, their weapons aimed at only the men.

"Ma'am, do you remember me?" Mage asked, as he knelt down on one knee in front of Edna.

"Yes, you are the police detective who told us that our neighbor was a murderer. I don't know why you are here, though. He's not here. He's next door," Edna told him, practically hyperventilating.

"We have reason to believe that he has been murdered and there are three men in this room who killed him," Mage told her.

"Please, she has terminal cancer. This is too much for her," Zayn said, concerned.

"That's one. Take him out of here," Mage said, directing officers to apprehend Zayn.

"No, he's my son. I need him to take care of me," Edna pleaded, rubbing the center of her chest.

"I will take care of you Edna," Frankie said, still

in a kneeling position on the floor with his hands behind his head.

"Shut up," one of the swat officers told Frankie, striking him at the base of his neck with the butt of his gun.

Frankie fell, face down on the floor at Edna's feet. Edna screamed as Frankie lay, unmoving.

"Stop, please don't hurt anyone else. I'm Silas Graham," Silas admitted.

"Get him out of here. Also, the one behind me is Jaxon Pierce," Mage informed. "The rest of you, I have a few questions."

"What about Frankie? I...think...he..." Edna began, before she passed out.

"We need paramedics in here," Mage requested, as he checked not only Edna's pulse, but also Frankie's.

"Is he going to be okay?" Derik asked.

"He's alive," Mage said, coldly.

"What is going on here? Are you going to tell us why you just barged in here and aimed guns at us?" Barry demanded.

"And why did you get aggressive with Frankie?"

Greg asked.

"For that matter, why was Silas, Zayn and Jaxon arrested?" Derik wanted to know.

The paramedics entered the house, as everyone other than Mage exited. Derik, Barry and Greg were led out to the driveway as Frankie and Edna were tended to.

"What the fuck is going on?" Derik asked, as Silas, Zayn and Jaxon were forced into the back seats of three different police cars.

"I have no idea. Why do they think they killed their neighbor?" Barry wondered.

"It doesn't make sense. There has to be some kind of mistake," Greg said.

"This is definitely a mistake. That guy probably left on his own and they have circumstantial evidence against them. Now they want us to say something they can use against them," Derik said.

"As a matter of fact, we have verbal confirmation of their planning of the murder," Mage informed them, as he joined them on the driveway.

"I doubt that," Derik spat.

"Would the three of you be willing to come down to the station to answer a few questions?" Mage requested.

"Fuck that! We are going to the hospital to make sure Frankie and Edna are okay. There was a better way to handle that situation," Derik told him, turning and walking to his vehicle.

"If you don't come down to the station now, I can always issue a warrant and have you brought to the station against your will," Mage said, raising his eyebrows.

"You can't do that," Derik said.

"As a matter of fact, I heard you telling your friends here about your involvement in the murder," Mage lied.

"You are a fucking asshole. Fine, we'll go answer your stupid questions, but I'm driving my own vehicle, so I can go to the hospital and check on Frankie when you are done," Derik agreed.

"That's a good boy. As a matter of fact, why don't you all arrive in the same vehicle. You can follow me there. And if at any time I think you are going to stray,

I will put a BOLO out on your vehicle so fast, you won't be able to make it a mile without being caught," Mage warned.

Derik, Barry and Greg climbed into Derik's single cab truck. Barry and Greg were glad that Derik had a bench seat, so the three of them could all sit next to each other. The ride to the police station was done in complete silence, as Derik was fuming and Barry and Greg were terrified at what had just occurred.

Twenty Three

Silas, Jaxon and Zayn were placed in three separate interrogation rooms, handcuffed to a metal bar attached to the table in front of them. The three of them had no intention of incriminating each other, nor themselves.

The only one that Silas was concerned about was

Frankie. He didn't deserve what happened to him.

"Your friends are telling us what happened, so you want to give me your side of the story?" Mage lied, as he entered the interrogation room with Silas.

"There isn't anything to tell, so I have nothing to say," Silas told him, sitting up straight and looking directly in front of him.

"Well, Zayn and Jaxon have already told us what happened, so you might as well corroborate their stories," Mage said.

"There isn't anything to tell, so I have nothing to say," Silas repeated, keeping his tone even.

"Okay, well I guess we aren't going to get anywhere," Mage said, opening the door to the room.

Mage allowed Derik to join Silas in the room. Immediately as soon as Silas saw Derik, his demeanor softened. Derik sat down across the table from Silas as Mage left the room.

"Silas, what the hell is going on?" Derik asked.

"I have no idea. This has to be some kind of misunderstanding. Zayn, Jaxon and I have nothing to do with whatever they seem to think happened to Evander," Silas told Derik.

"Why do they think you did?"

"Detective Mage believes there is some kind of recording of the three of us talking about how we would kill him."

"Three men standing around talking about how they would kill someone, doesn't say they did. How can they prove it?"

"They don't have anything. At this point we have only been arrested and we are being detained. There isn't anything to charge us with."

"I finally have the opportunity to be with you and this whole thing has just thrown a wrench in our plans," Derik said, reaching across the table to hold Silas' hands.

"Our plans haven't changed. As soon as I am released, we will move into my house together," Silas told him, leaning his head down to press his lips against Derik's hands.

"Alright, that's enough," Mage said, bursting into the room, sounding defeated. "The chief says I have to let you go. Jaxon and Zayn are already waiting with

Barry and Greg."

"I told you there was no reason for you to hold us here," Silas said, as Mage unlocked and removed the handcuffs.

"Can we go see Frankie and Edna in the hospital now?" Derik requested, as he stepped up next to the others with Silas.

"Yes please," they all said, simultaneously.

"Oh, gentlemen," Mage addressed the group. "Keep in mind, that as soon as I can prove that the three of you have killed Evander, I'll be coming back for you."

"As long as the next time you have a wild theory that causes you to burst into my home, you don't injure any innocent people," Silas told him.

The group of men headed out of the police station and into the parking lot. As they noticed Derik's three seater truck, Silas, Jaxon and Zayn decided to ride in the bed of the truck, while Derik, Barry and Greg rode in the cab.

On the ride to the hospital, Silas, Zayn and Jaxon discussed what they talked about in their individual interrogation rooms. They were all relieved when they were released.

"Mage tried to tell me that y'all were telling him everything that we had done, so I needed to start talking," Silas told them.

"He told me the same thing," Zayn replied.

"That's what he told me," Jaxon revealed.

"So he was trying to pit us against each other, in order to find out who would crack first," Silas said.

"I didn't say anything," Zayn said.

"Neither did I," Jaxon said.

"Nor did I," Silas said. "If either of us admitted to killing Evander, we would also have to reveal the other murders each of us had committed and there is no way in hell I'm going to tell anyone else about that."

"I agree. I think we all need a hiatus until Mage moves on," Zayn said.

Twenty Four

As soon as Derik parked the truck in the lot at the hospital, they all piled out and rushed in. Zayn and Jaxon went to Edna first, while Silas, Barry, Greg and Derik went to Frankie.

Frankie was awake, but seemed confused as to what was going on around him. He was, however, glad to see his friends.

"What happened?" Frankie asked.

"What is the last thing you remember?" Barry asked, holding Frankie's hand.

"I remember the police storming into Silas' house, but after that, I'm not sure what happened," Frankie revealed.

"Well, how are you feeling?" Silas asked.

"Other than the monster headache, I have a bald spot on the back of my head with a bandage covering what they told me was a severe laceration that required seventeen stitches," Frankie said.

"I'm so sorry, Frankie. Please forgive me," Silas told him, stepping up to the bed and wrapping his arms around Frankie's neck.

"It's not your fault. Unless you caused the wound to the back of my head," Frankie said, hugging Silas back.

"No, he didn't do anything. There is a crazy police detective who was investigating his next door neighbor, when all of a sudden, now the neighbor is missing. Somehow, this detective has it in his head that he has some recording of Silas, Jaxon and Zayn discussing how they were going to murder their neighbor," Derik said.

"That doesn't mean they killed him," Frankie said.

"That's what I told the detective. I asked him if there was any evidence in the...Silas, what's your neighbor's name?" Derik asked.

"Evander," Silas told him, finally releasing Frankie from his embrace.

"Evander. I asked the detective if there was any evidence in Evander's house to suggest that he was dead. When he told me no, they only had the alleged recording, which was obtained illegally, I walked over and spoke with the chief. After that, the detective allowed me to go into the interrogation room with Silas, then the chief forced the detective to let the guys go," Derik explained.

"Sounds like that detective has something against you guys. Maybe he's mad that y'all are better looking than he is," Frankie laughed.

"Yeah, I'm sure that's what it is. I'm so glad that you are doing okay. You don't mind if I go check on

Edna, do you?" Silas asked Frankie.

"What happened to Edna?" Frankie wanted to know, trying to get out of the bed.

"Whoa, just hold on. You can't get up," Derik said, attempting to hold him down to the bed.

"I want to know what happened to Edna," Frankie argued, struggling under his four friends doing what they could to keep him from getting up.

Greg walked out of the room for a few moments, then returned with a nurse. The nurse had a needle in her hand, that was filled about a quarter of the way with a clear liquid.

"Okay, Frankie. I'm going to give you something to calm down," the nurse told him, inserting the needle into his IV and injecting the clear liquid into it.

"How long is that going to take to go into effect. We don't want him to injure himself," Barry asked the nurse.

"It won't take long," she said, just as Frankie stopped struggling and relaxed back onto the bed.

"Just relax hun," the nurse told Frankie.

The nurse left the room, after checking Frankie's

blood pressure and pulse. Frankie was subdued and relaxed, but conscious. Barry, Greg, Silas and Derik backed away from Frankie, just as he sunk back onto the bed and cuddled under the blanket.

"I am going to go check on Edna and I will be right back and I promise, I will fill you in on how she is doing," Silas told Frankie.

"You better come back," was all Frankie said, before closing his eyes and falling asleep.

"I'll go with you. Barry and Greg, stay here with Frankie. We'll be right back," Derik said, as he headed out the door behind Silas.

"I think Frankie is going to be just fine, but I still feel bad that this happened to him," Silas told Derik, as they walked down the hall toward Edna's room.

"This was not your fault. Please stop blaming yourself. I think we should help Frankie get a lawyer and sue the police. This should have never happened," Derik said.

"I agree. We should bring this up to the chief and inform him that we are planning to sue, unless Detective Mage is transferred out of that department and stays away from us," Silas agreed, as they stepped up to the room Edna was in.

Derik knocked softly, before he slowly opened the door. The light was dim in the room and the curtains were drawn to block out the parking and street lights.

"Hello," Silas said, softly.

"Silas, Derik, how is Frankie?" Edna asked, from the bed.

"He's really worried about you," Derik told her.

"I'm trying to see if I can switch rooms, so I can be in the room with him," Edna said.

"How are you feeling?" Silas asked.

"I'm fine. I just had a panic attack, which caused my blood pressure to rise and I passed out. It's not that big of a deal, but because of the cancer that has taken over my body, they want to keep me here until my next chemo treatment," Edna informed.

"The nurse had to subdue Frankie when he found out you were also here. He tried to get out of the bed and was fighting to leave the room, so we had to request assistance to keep him in the room," Derik told her.

"That's it," Edna said, pressing the call button on the bed remote.

Within a few moments, a nurse entered the room. She first checked Edna's vital signs before asking what she needed.

"I need you to either move me to Frankie's room, or move Frankie into my room. I need it done within the next ten minutes, or I will be contacting my oncologist and make sure that I'm released, so I can go to his room," Edna ordered the nurse.

"I'll see what I can do," the nurse said, rolling her eyes.

"You better make it happen," Edna yelled, as the nurse stepped out into the hall.

Eventually, Edna was able to be moved into Frankie's room and they were both released within a couple days.

Twenty Five

The day that Frankie and Edna were released from the hospital, the entire group headed down to the police station to speak with the chief of police. The fact that swat had stormed Silas' house specifically for Silas, Zayn and Jaxon, but two innocent bystanders were hospitalized due to the negligence of one detective, they wanted to make sure it wouldn't happen again.

"I want to know what is being done about Detective Mage. We would have been more than willing to come down here to speak with him if he had requested," Zayn insisted, holding Edna's hand.

"I understand everyone's concern. The situation could have been handled differently and I agree there was no reason that he should have involved the swat team," the chief agreed.

"Detective Mage needs to be disciplined for his role in Frankie's injury," Silas told him.

"He has been suspended for seven days. We are taking this situation very seriously." The chief's answers seemed scripted.

"We know our houses were searched. They have been trashed and our belongings have been thrown around. Were they able to find what they were looking for?" Zayn asked.

Derik had taken Silas, Jaxon and Zayn home to shower and change their clothes after Edna had been moved into Frankie's hospital room. That's when the three of them found their homes had been raided and everything had been thrown around. They helped each other clean up their homes, before they headed back to the hospital, each in their own vehicles.

"There wasn't any evidence found in any of the four homes, including Mr. Thomson's, that would suggest any type of crime happened. I apologize for what happened to all of you, but what exactly is it that you expect me to do?" the chief said, irritated.

"First, we want to be sure that Detective Mage will no longer bother us and all of Frankie and Edna's medical bills from their hospital stay due to his negligence are taken care of by you. If refused, we will turn to the legal system and request a whole lot more as compensation," Silas demanded, slamming his hand down on the desk.

"I can assure you that Detective Mage will be heavily reprimanded and ordered to leave you all alone. As for medical expenses, I will see what I can do," the chief told them.

"Keep us informed. If we see Detective Mage parked on our street, or anywhere in our neighborhood, we will file harassment charges against him," Zayn threatened.

With that, they all stood to leave, as the chief of police lowered his head in defeat. Barry and Greg rode with Derik, as Frankie rode with Silas in order to retrieve their vehicles from Silas' home.

"Do you really think Mage will follow the orders to leave y'all alone?" Frankie asked Silas during the drive.

"No, I think he will most likely show up at some point, off the clock, just to keep an eye on us," Silas told him.

"Why does he think you guys murdered Evander?"

"He was supposedly surveilling Evander as a possible serial killer and continuously questioned us because we were his neighbors. Mage wanted to know if we had seen anything suspicious. When we didn't give him the answers he was looking for, I can only assume, that was when he decided to stake out the entire cul-de-sac. I don't know what caused him to believe that Evander had been murdered. For all we know, he's at home."

"It just doesn't make any sense. If he originally was looking at Evander, what in the world caused him to believe that he had been murdered? And why would he think that you guys did it?" Frankie asked, confused.

"I don't know. We told Mage that we didn't really get along with Evander, so we didn't know too much about him," Silas told him.

"I just don't understand why he would turn his focus to you three guys," Frankie said, more as an observation.

"Shit Frankie, we don't know!" Silas yelled.

"Okay, gees."

Frankie decided to continue the ride in silence. He had never known Silas to be so aggressive and decided that his outburst was out of frustration.

Silas realized that his anger was misplaced. "I'm sorry Frankie. I don't mean to snap at you, but this entire situation is…what the fuck!"

As Silas turned down the cul-de-sac toward his home, he noticed Mage's black vehicle parked out in front of Evander's home. He swung his vehicle into his driveway, with Derik, Barry and Greg behind him.

Opening his driver's side door and exiting the vehicle without turning off the engine, Silas stormed over to the black car. He pounded on the driver's side window in order to get the detective's attention.

"What the fuck are you doing here?" Silas yelled, as Mage rolled down the window.

"Calm down Mr. Graham. I can still contact dispatch and have you arrested," Mage said, calmly.

"You are not to be here, or bother us. You need to leave before I contact the chief and have you removed," Silas warned.

"Do what you think you have to do, but right now, I'm just waiting for Mr. Thomson to return home," Mage lied.

Detective Mage felt as though if he could prove Silas, Zayn and Jaxon were actually involved with the reason Evander couldn't be located, he would be seen as a hero rather than the station's screw-up. He was offended that he had been suspended due to the swat team being aggressive.

"I'm calling the police," Edna's small voice warned, after Zayn had returned home with her.

"I know you guys are involved somehow. I haven't been able to get in touch with Mr. Thomson since our last discussion. You revealed that he had ruined an important moment for you, but I wasn't able to find out what that was. Due to that statement, I placed a listening device under your dining room table in order to find out what the specific moment was.

"While I was listening to you guys planning the murder of Mr. Thomson, to which you revealed that you all knew he was a killer, I found out about a man who had been brutally sodomized and stabbed about two hundred miles from here. The DNA evidence found on the man's body matched that of Mr. Thomson. Once I was able to obtain an arrest warrant, that was when he was no longer able to be located and I turned my sights on the three of you," Mage admitted.

"Maybe Evander was aware that you were on to him and he fled the area," Derik claimed, as he stepped up behind Silas and wrapped his arms around Silas's waist.

Jaxon had arrived home at that time and everyone was now gathered around the detective's car. Mage was calm and seemed to think he was smarter than the other men. Edna remained on the driveway of Zayn's home on the phone with the police.

"I heard them planning to murder their neighbor," Mage told Derik.

"And you weren't that slick in thinking that we didn't see you place the device under the table," Zayn lied.

"What do you mean?" Mage wondered.

"We saw you stick something under the table. It was our idea to mess with you. Unfortunately, we underestimated the fact that you would barge into Silas' home while we were having a get-together with other people to which you would cause injury," Jaxon told Mage.

"That's not true. I heard you. You all were talking about how you were going to kill him and the fact that you all had your own kill styles and wanted to kill him to match his own kill style," Mage said, like a child trying to explain how the situation wasn't his fault.

"Detective, have you ever known more than one serial killer to live within the vicinity of each other, let alone four," Barry said, seeing the ridiculousness of what Mage had stated.

Silas' friends laughed at the situation, as Silas, Zayn and Jaxon realized that they could keep their secret from everyone else in their lives. No one believed that they were killers and they planned to keep it that way. Before Mage could respond to Barry, police sirens could be heard in the distance.

"They are coming for you, Detective. I suggest you take this as a sign to leave us alone and never come back," Silas told him, raising his eyebrows.

"I'm going to wait. I believe they are coming for you," Mage said, leaning back in his seat and crossing his arms over his chest.

Everyone backed away from Mage's vehicle and headed over to stand on Silas' driveway, as several patrol vehicles turned the corner with their sirens blaring. They surrounded Mage's car, before the sirens were silenced. Not only did uniformed officers exit the patrol vehicles, but so did the chief of police.

"Mage, turn off your vehicle and toss your keys out of the window," the chief ordered.

"No, arrest them," Mage practically whined.

"Mage, there isn't any proof that they have done anything wrong," the chief said.

"I gave you the recordings I had of them talking about murdering their neighbor. They planned it and now he can't be located," Mage pleaded.

"We haven't found any evidence to suggest that these men have done anything wrong. I also spoke to Mr. Thomson's parents who informed me that he is notorious for disappearing if at any point he thinks he is in trouble," the chief informed.

"Then why is his truck still here?" Mage asked.

"His parents told me that is for appearances. He was most likely picked up by one of his friends and he is probably hiding out somewhere. Now please, exit the vehicle and come with us."

"Am I going to be arrested?"

"No, not arrested, but IA would like to talk to you about your future as a detective."

"If internal affairs wants to talk to me, then I'm

probably going to be fired."

"Most likely they would just transfer you to a different department, so this doesn't happen again. Now please, follow my instructions and get out of the car," the chief demanded.

"No, I'm not going down like this. If I'm transferred out of homicide, that means I will end up either in cold cases or vice and both of those departments are practically a demotion," Mage said, retrieving his side arm from his hip holster.

"He's got a gun, he's got a gun!" one uniformed officer yelled.

All of the officers ducked behind their vehicles with their service weapons drawn. Zayn ran across the street to protect his mother, while the others ducked around Silas's garage in order to hide on his front porch.

"I would rather go down as a homicide detective, than to retire as a miserable old man," Mage said, as he lifted the gun to the side of his head.

"Mage, put the gun down. Don't do this," the chief begged.

Mage closed his eyes and whispered a little prayer. He took a deep breath, before dropping his hand down onto the passenger seat next to him and allowing the gun to fall out of his hand.

Twenty Six

The chief of police and the uniformed officers frantically ran up to Mage's vehicle, as he opened the door. Mage was pulled from his vehicle and placed face down in the grass. One uniformed officer kneeled on Mage's tailbone, as he was handcuffed. Two other uniformed officers linked their arms with Mage and lifted him into a standing position, once the other officer had removed his knee.

"What were you thinking?" the chief asked Mage.

"I'm telling you there is something about these guys. They are killers and I intend to prove it!" Mage yelled, trying to lunge at the guys who were standing on Silas' driveway at that point.

"Are you guys okay?" the chief asked them.

"We are fine. This is crazy. We don't understand why he is trying to pin a crime on us," Jaxon wondered.

"I don't know why he thinks as though you guys have anything to do with Mr. Thomson's disappearance. I just hope that he takes this entire experience and you guys will now be left alone. I'm sorry you all have had to deal with this. Due to his actions, we have to take this situation seriously. I will be requesting a search warrant for Mr. Thomson's home and soon the street will be swarming with crime scene investigators. I will need y'all to go inside, just to be out of the way. If we need you for anything, I will personally come to speak with you," the chief said.

The men all headed across the street to join up with Zayn and Edna. Zayn was standing on his driveway and entered the house as the group followed him in.

"What happened? Who was shouting?" Edna asked, as Zayn closed the front door after everyone had joined her in the living room.

"Detective Mage was just arrested and he was yelling at us," Frankie told her, cuddling up on the sofa with her.

"What!" Edna exclaimed. "Why was he yelling at y'all."

"Apparently the guy is crazy. Of course we all already knew that," Derik said, cuddling up with Silas.

"Well, I guess that means we are off the hook," Jaxon said.

"What do you mean, 'off the hook'? We weren't on the hook for anything," Zayn said, punching Jaxon's bicep.

"I just mean we aren't being looked into for something we didn't do." Jaxon tried to save face.

"What is going on out there right now?" Edna

asked.

"Crime scene investigation," Barry told her.

"What crime scene? Nothing happened. The crazy detective made something up in his head. They shouldn't need to investigate," Edna scoffed.

"They are going to investigate Evander's house. I guess for now we are going to have to stay here until they are done," Silas said.

"Well then, who's going to make dinner?" Edna said, nudging Frankie.

"I got you, Momma Edna," Frankie agreed, jumping up and heading toward the kitchen, with Zayn behind him for assistance.

As they were cleaning up after dinner, the chief of police knocked on the door. Zayn walked over and opened the door.

"Thank y'all so much for allowing us to take over your street. You are now free to return to your homes," the chief told them.

"Did you find any evidence to prove that the three of us murdered Evander?" Silas asked, crossing his arms over his chest as he stepped up behind Zayn.

"We didn't find anything that may have suggested Evander was murdered at all. He may have just left on his own accord once he noticed Detective Mage was surveilling him," the chief informed them.

"So what do we do about Detective Mage now?" Jaxon wanted to know, standing behind Silas.

"We will take care of Detective Mage. Y'all can continue your lives as normal," the chief reassured them.

Silas, Zayn and Jaxon shook hands with the chief of police and thanked him. The three men went back to their friends and family before all going home for the night.

Twenty Seven

Three months later, Frankie, Barry and Greg were helping Derik move into Silas' home. Silas and Derik's relationship was progressing and they were excited to take the next step.

Silas no longer had the urge to engage in autoerotic asphyxiation and he was satisfied with his choice to proceed with the relationship. His needs were being met by Derik and he no longer felt the urge to kill.

Zayn had decided to take the year off from eliminating domestic abusers and try to form a more romantic relationship with his lady friend. She had been the wife of one of the men that Zayn had murdered. She had pursued him after her husband disappeared and she was afraid of being alone.

As for Jaxon, he continued bringing home vagrants and runaways, mixing their bodies into his fertilizer pile. He didn't see a reason to stop, considering that he didn't have the urge to have a relationship with anyone, nor did he feel the need for connection.

The chief of police had called to inform the men that Mage had been released after being relieved of duty. Silas felt as though nothing would keep Mage from stalking the cul-de-sac. It didn't matter that he was no longer a police officer, his obsession would draw him in.

"Maybe we should file for a restraining order," Zayn suggested, as the three of them stood in the kitchen of Jaxon's house.

"I don't think that would help," Silas said.

"I agree. If Mage wants to watch us, just let him. He won't be able to prove anything," Jaxon said, confidently.

"You are the only one who would go down if he did decide to continue watching us," Zayn told Jaxon.

"He would only assume that I run a boarding house. He wouldn't be able to prove that they didn't leave," Jaxon said.

"You don't think that he would be suspicious that more people are entering your house, than are leaving?" Silas asked.

"He has to sleep and leave to eat sometime. I could just say that they left when he wasn't looking," Jaxon said, shrugging his shoulders and smiling.

"Well, you just seem to have this all figured out," Zayn said, rolling his eyes.

"Right now I think we just need to focus on our lives and hope that Mage doesn't return," Silas said.

"What is Derik doing right now?" Jaxon asked, trying to change the subject.

"He's organizing the house. I told him that it was

his decision as to what furniture we kept and what needed to go, so he is making that choice now. He is also putting away all the stuff from his boxes," Silas told them.

"He doesn't want your help?" Jaxon asked.

"Derik is very particular," Silas informed.

"Well let's go see if maybe he would like any assistance," Jaxon said.

Silas, Zayn and Jaxon headed for the front door. Just as Jaxon placed his hand on the door knob, they heard a knock. Jaxon opened the door and Mage stood on the other side.

"What the hell are you doing here?" Silas yelled.

"Your boyfriend told me that y'all were here. I just wanted to let you know that I intend to prove that the three of you are killers and I will expose you to the world," Mage said, pointing his finger at them.

"The whole world, huh. Well, I hope you get an award for it," Zayn told him.

"You guys are killers and I know I can prove it!" Mage yelled and stomped his foot before turning and walking back to his car, which was parked in his stake out spot at the end of the road.

"Wow. He is really hard pressed to pin something on us," Silas said.

"Thank goodness we don't do anything suspicious," Jaxon laughed.

"Technically, Silas and I don't do anything suspicious here at home. You on the other hand, bringing home vagrants who never leave, that's suspicious," Zayn told Jaxon.

"Whatever. Get out of my house," Jaxon said jokingly, ushering the guys out the front door, before closing it behind him.

Derik was standing on the driveway of Silas' house, looking at the black car parked at the curb, basically in front of the house. Silas, Zayn and Jaxon walked over and stood next to Derik.

"Is that the car that Detective Mage is driving? I thought he was suppose to leave y'all alone?" Derik asked.

"Apparently he still believes something sinister happened to Evander and he is obsessed with proving it," Jaxon said.

"I will tell you this much Jaxon, you are the first on his radar. He just came over here asking me about the smell of decomposition coming from your home," Derik told him.

"He came over and talked to you?" Silas asked.

"Yeah. He knocked on the door shortly after you left to go over to Jaxon's house," Derik replied.

"That smell is that of dead animals. I mix road kill into my fertilizer pile in my back yard. Sometimes the smell can be overwhelming, but I don't know what I can do to fix it," Jaxon said.

"You might want to do something. That smell is pretty overwhelming and when the wind shifts I can smell it *in* my house," Zayn told Jaxon.

"Maybe we could manufacture a perfume to add to the chemical mixture you have to assist in the decomposition, in order to mask the smell," Silas suggested.

"That's a great idea. I was mixing fruit garbage in at one time, but it no longer masks the smell. Do you have any idea on how to do that?" Jaxon asked.

"Possibly. We can try a few different combinations in order to get it just right," Silas said. "The smell does seem to be getting stronger. It's almost as if you have added more animals in the past few weeks than ever before."

"I may have. There have been more animals that I have found on the side of the road lately," Jaxon said, shrugging.

"Isn't manure better as fertilizer than rotting animal carcasses?" Derik wondered.

"Manure is the base in my fertilizer. Mostly pig shit. A few times there was pig pieces, like hooves and snout, mixed into the manure delivery. Those times, it seemed my clients lawns flourished. After that, I just kept adding dead things to the pile and my business has never been more profitable," Jaxon informed Derik.

"Okay, y'all go fix that," Derik said, as the wind shifted and wafted the smell in their direction.

"Let me go inside to get a few things and I'll meet you guys over at Jaxon's house to try to fix this situation," Silas said, walking toward his front door.

"If Zayn can smell that inside *his* house, I can only imagine what it smells like in *your* house. I have been over here before and it has never been this strong," Derik said, waving his hand in front of his face.

Jaxon shrugged. "I guess I'm just use to the smell."

"I don't know how anyone could get use to that smell. Come on killer," Zayn joked, leading Jaxon toward his house.

"I'm going to get you!" Mage yelled, standing outside his vehicle, leaning against the driver's side door.

"Prove it, bitch!" Jaxon yelled back, as he walked backwards toward his home.

"Ignore him. Just go inside the house and pretend like he isn't there," Zayn told Jaxon.

Derik turned and walked into the house, just as Silas was on his way out. The two lovers shared a passionate kiss, before Silas headed over to Jaxon's house.

"I have a few things here that we can try. I brought candles and some little jars of some scented oils that Frankie keeps bringing over. He says with Derik living there, he wants to make sure the house doesn't smell like sex when he comes over," Silas scoffed, placing the items on the counter in Jaxon's kitchen.

"Frankie is a real pip," Zayn said.

"Okay grandpa," Jaxon told Zayn, as the three of them laughed.

Outside Jaxon's house, Mage had retrieved a bottle of whiskey and an oily rag from the trunk of his car. He walked toward the house and stood in the street, at the bottom of the driveway.

"Okay killers! Come out here right now," Mage yelled.

"What the hell is he doing?" Silas asked.

"Who cares, just ignore him," Zayn said.

"This shit is getting out of hand. I'm calling the police," Jaxon said, grabbing his phone.

"I'm going to fucking kill you guys for getting me fired!" Mage yelled.

Mage walked up the driveway and stood just outside the living room window, as he took the top off the bottle and stuffed a quarter of the rag down into the opening. He pulled a lighter out of his pocket and lit the rag on fire.

Once it was flaming, Mage hurled the bottle through the front window and watched as the fire raged through the room. He ran back to his vehicle as he heard the men inside scrambling. In the back seat, Mage had retrieved an oxygen tank. Quickly, he ran back toward the house as Jaxon opened the front door.

"What the fuck are you doing!" Jaxon yelled.

Silas, Zayn and Jaxon were standing in the doorway, flames raging behind them, as Mage tossed the oxygen tank at them. Jaxon caught the container as Mage backed away pulling out a 9mm Glock from the holster on his hip. Once he felt he was a safe distance away, Mage took aim and shot the oxygen tank.

The three men, along with Jaxon's home, was engulfed in flames. The explosion shook the ground beneath Mage's feet, as he walked back toward his vehicle, grinning from ear to ear. He backed his vehicle down the street and drove off, just as Edna and Derik emerged from their homes to investigate the tragedy.

C. L. Conolly is the author of several horror novels. She has been writing stories since the age of six and after graduating high school, she then went on to gain an MFA in Creative Writing. She has studied the sadistic minds of the most infamous serial killers as well as police and crime scene procedures in order to write accurately.

C. L. Conolly prefers writing long hand by putting pen to paper. When she is not writing, she enjoys reading, crocheting and spending time with her family.

Facebook: C. L. Conolly - Author
TikTok: C. L. Conolly
Instagram: clconolly
YouTube: C. L. Conolly
Twitter: CLConolly

KILLER
WORDS
PUBLISHING